I0824680

PIXIE FOLK TALES

HENRY EVERETT

First published 2025

The History Press
97 St George's Place, Cheltenham,
Gloucestershire, GL50 3QB
www.thehistorypress.co.uk

British Library Cataloguing in Publication Data.
A catalogue record for this book is available from the British Library.

ISBN 978 1 80399 616 5

Typesetting and origination by The History Press.
Printed and bound in Great Britain by TJ Books, Padstow, Cornwall.

The History Press proudly supports
Trees for Life
www.treesforlife.org.uk

EU Authorised Representative: Easy Access System Europe
Mustamäe tee 50, 10621 Tallinn, Estonia
gpst.request@easproject.com

Dedicated to my grannie, Poppet Hall.
Through her company and garden I knew magic.

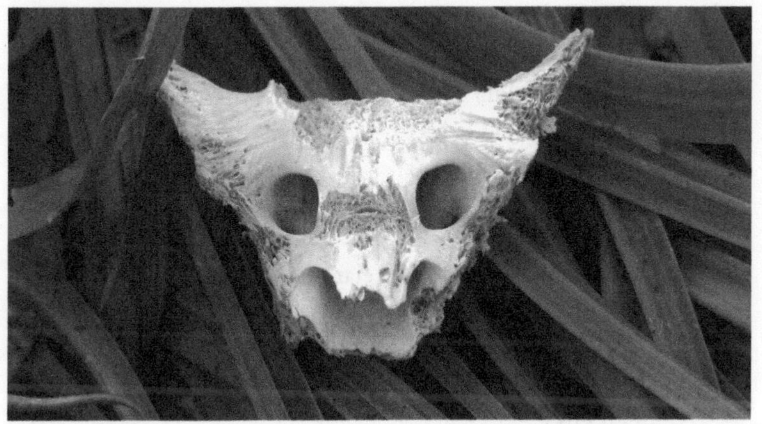

CONTENTS

ACKNOWLEDGEMENTS

Massive thanks to Nicola Guy at The History Press for trusting me with this project and to David Wyatt for his wonderful illustrations; thank you for bringing these tales to life.

Huge thank you to Lisa Schneidau for her unwavering support, encouragement and wisdom. Thank you to Ronnie Conboy, Sara Hurley and everyone who has shared stories at South Devon Storytellers. Thank you to Sharon Jacksties and Jem Dick for introducing me to Somerset with such warmth, and to Mike and Tina O'Connor for the long hours of most wonderful conversation.

Thank you to John Buckingham, whose love for Nellie Sloggett brought her to life, and to Pete Ward, whose relationship with the land continually inspires me. Thank you to my Pixie friends Lu Christie and Claire Casely and to Holly Ebony for allowing her song to be included in these pages.

This book would not have been possible without Simon Young, Alex Langstone, Rupert White, John Kruse and Jeremy Harte.

Thank you Anna, Bex and Julia for feeding me in the final hours! And thank you to Tim and Jess Graves for giving me time to finish the book.

Dad, Jenny, Romilly, Sam, Tobin, Elowyn, Doug, Neesha, Poppie, Pippin and Pooka. I love you.

To each Pixie that lured me!
To each place that held me!
To each story that fed me!

Welcome to Pixieland!

HOW I MET THE PIXIES

I was lucky enough to grow up surrounded by fields on the edge of a village on Dartmoor. My siblings and I played outside for hours at a time. We made dens in the tall grass and base camps beneath the trees and followed paths in the hedges. We walked the old lanes along rivers filled with mossy boulders and explored the open moor.

I left the country to go to university, then moved to the city. More than a decade later, during a year in Australia, I was reminded with ferocity how alive the earth really is. Australia is loud! In bird and insect, stone and water. In colour, temperature, mass and volume. It blew me away.

I was introduced to the artwork and traditional stories of the First Nations people. Although I do not profess to comprehend the depth of their visual and cultural narrative, I was amazed how both felt alive with spirit. So much so, that it felt *part* of the living landscape.

I returned to England not sure I had ever seen anything of British traditional culture that felt as deep or in harmony with the land as I had seen in Australia.

What were the traditional stories of my home? Had we sold it all under capitalism? Is this why our western world is so fragmented from the environment? Is this how we have come to be facing environmental collapse?

I returned to Devon, to the village I grew up in. I walked extensively and discovered something amazing one day. On Dartmoor, I walked past a puddle that had submerged stones in it. On a whim of fancy, I thought it looked like a dragon's nest. That evening, by chance, I met storyteller Sara Hurley. I told her about the dragon's nest and she told me that I must already know the legend of the dragon from that part of the moor; I did not. Funnily enough, the story was of a man who found a dragon's nest just a mile from where I had been. I became obsessed with this story and the idea that perhaps the land really *does* want us to engage with it. To step into our imaginations and … listen! To give it personhood, to treat it with respect and offer it our service.

Sara invited me to South Devon Storytellers, a local story circle, where traditional stories are shared informally. I was enchanted by performance storytellers who breathed life into old tales. The room came to life and my imagination transported me across landscapes, into the depths of magic, danger and wisdom, before returning me back into my body again. I had been writing stories and poems for a few years, but I had never experienced story like this. These stories were medicines of adventure, wisdom and knowledge, surprise, wonder and fun. They shone a light on to what I was looking for.

As a teenager, *Faeries* by Brian Froud and Alan Lee had a profound influence on me, as I sought out stories of the land, I returned to the Fae. Pixies have always been my local mischievous characters, hiding in the hills. I knew their mischief, but I didn't know their stories. So I started looking. It felt like the Pixies heard my longing to meet the land and their tales.

So began many adventures across Dartmoor, wider Devon, Cornwall and Somerset. As I delved into stories and places, Lisa Schneidau taught me that if you want to learn a story, 'walk with it'. It feels to me that stories really live outside, held between people and place. Outside you can meet the mystery of being, internally and externally. In this way, I started walking with the Pixies.

Pareidolia is the term given to the tendency to perceive patterns or images in random or ambiguous stimuli. Whilst exploring the places where the Pixie tales herald from, I caught endless glimpses of smiling faces in stones, in the leaves of trees or floating on the river surface. Every glimpse felt like I had discovered a Pixie treasure and made my adventures feel even more mischievous and playful, so within these pages I have included many of my own photographs of these 'Pixie treasures'. It is a glorious reminder that the way we see the world defines how we colour our experience. Our imagination truly is a gateway – if you look for magic, the face of magic will look for you!

The book in your hands has been a magical adventure. The stories have had a profound effect upon me. I am retelling them to you, so that they can spread their magic and enchant *your* story. But let us not forget the generations of people who have passed on these stories; their words are not forgotten.

Because the folk tale is an inherited cultural tradition, I have focused on folk tales for this volume. I am leaving out many authored tales, and, aside from some exceptions, personal accounts, which are both fascinating and illuminating. For anyone interested in further reading, I have included a bibliography and reading list.

But, a warning. Something serious. Be aware.

The book in your hands is filled with pages of the enchantments of the Pixies. These beings want to dance into your imagination. They will call you to the magic that awaits, inside and outside. Be warned, they are experts at leading people astray. They will laugh and they will clap when they lead you into boggy terrain. Be careful how you go.

This book is aimed at adults. I advise caution before opening a story at random and reading it to a child.

The Pixies' stories have changed my life … do not think they won't do the same for you.

Expect enchantment!

WHO ARE THE PIXIES?

Pixies and Fairies are creatures we meet either by extraordinary encounter, or through story. Pixie and Fairy are often interchangeable terms in modern society. What are the boundaries between them? What defines one from the other?

In 1953, Disney created some confusion with his depiction of Tinkerbell in his animated version of J.M. Barrie's *Peter Pan*. The story started as a play in 1904 and became a book in 1911. Tinkerbell had been written as a Fairy; the idea she was a Pixie did not come along until Disney released his film.

> All it takes is faith and trust, oh and something I forgot! Dust! Just a little bit of Pixie dust!
>
> *Peter Pan*, Disney (1953)

In the film, Tinkerbell is referred to as a Pixie by Wendy, Michael, Hook and Smee. Peter tells the children that Tink's 'Pixie Dust', will give them the ability to fly. To confuse the matter further, Disney designed Tinkerbell as a typical-looking Fairy. The release of *Peter Pan* was significantly delayed, but the concept drawings of Tinkerbell were envisioned as early as 1935, while the Blue Fairy (of *Pinocchio*, 1940) and Sugar Plum Fairies (of *Fantasia*, 1940) were in studio production.

However, we cannot blame Disney entirely. Georgian and Victorian depictions of Fairies were rife with small-winged spirits. In his 1793 poem 'Song of the Pixies', Samuel Taylor Coleridge described his spirits with 'filmy pinion' (insect-like wings). Since Shakespeare, depictions of Fairies have taken whatever image suits the audience at the time. Shakespeare was the first to miniaturise Fairies. To add to the problem, Fairy can refer to an individual, but it can also be used as an umbrella term to refer to a wide range of magical beings.

To understand what makes a Pixie, we must visit the sources of their folk legend, which takes us to South West England. In the folk collections of Cornwall, Devon and Somerset we find the surviving folk tales of the Pixies.

As we will see in 'Battle of Pixies and Fairies', Pixies claimed the territory of 'Pixieland' as everything west of the River Parrett to Land's End. Within this boundary, the majority of Pixie stories are to be found.

Piskey, Pisgie, Pixie, Pigsey, Pixey and Pixy are all used. In their stories, I have used the spelling we find in their original sources, but I use Pixie throughout for simplicity. I have chosen to capitalise their names to honour their personhood.

Some folklorists have insisted that there are clear differences and identifiable types of Pixie within the South West. What defines a Pixie, it seems, has always been up for debate. However, these characteristics are worth noting.

As we begin this journey, it is only proper and polite for me to introduce you to the magical folk you can expect to meet along our adventure.

Welcome to Pixieland.

Pixies or Pigsies (sometimes Piskies)

West Country Fairies are usually depicted as elven beings of the hobgoblin family. Usually wearing green, naked or dressed as a bundle of rags. Often found in Somerset with red hair and squinty eyes, sometimes wearing red caps. Lovers of music and dancing, water and solitary places. Generally depicted standing anywhere between eight inches to three feet tall, occasionally human size.

Particularly fond of misleading travellers, stealing horses and riding them in circles.

Sometimes explained as souls of heathens, not permitted entry into heaven, or as souls of infants who died before baptism (Bray, Vol. 1, 1836, p.172).

Piskeys

The Cornish Piskey is similar to the Pixie in Somerset and Devon.

Hunt believed Piskeys belonged to an older family than those in Devonshire. Katherine Briggs agreed, stating the Cornish Piskey is 'older, more wizened and meagre than the sturdy, earth Pixies of Somerset and the white, slight, naked Pixies of Devon.' (Briggs, 1976, p.328)

Knockers

Knockers are found working in Cornish mines; they are often male, diminished characters, usually with beards. Some believed they were the souls of Jews, eternally bound to work in the mines for a supposed role in the crucifixion.

Imps, Gathorns, Buccas, Nickers, Nuggies and Spriggans are all names used to describe those who frequent Cornish mines (Wright, 1914, p.199).

Spriggans

Spriggans are known as the most dangerous spirits in Cornwall. Often referred to as grotesque with crooked features, the sight of a Spriggan was said to be terrifying. Spriggans are thieves who hoard stolen treasure; they are even responsible for stealing children and leaving changelings. Bottrell tells us they could blight crops and create whirlwinds to make mischief. Hunt tells us they are the spirits of Giants who have diminished. When angered they can grow to Giant proportions to frighten intruders. Because of this, they are also seen as guardians of the Piskey doors.

Bucca

Possibly related to Pooka (Ireland) and Pwcca (Wales), Bucca is a shapeshifter, sometimes appearing as a black buck goat, an aquatic being, or a mining spirit. Bucca appears frequently in West Penwith. Botterell referred to Bucca as an 'ancient divinity'.

'Fisherman left a portion of their catch on the sand for Bucca, and in harvest a piece of bread at lunch-time was thrown over the left shoulder, and a few drops of beer spilt on the ground for him, to ensure good luck.' (Courtney, 1890, p.129)

People referred to Bucca Gwidder (white) and Bucca Dhu/Boo (black), the former benevolent, the latter malevolent. Bucca Boo became synonymous with the devil, and in some tales appears as Old Nick. Bucca can also mean 'fool'.

The Small People/The Little Folk/Pobel Vean

The Small People are thought to be the spirits of ancestors who inhabited Cornwall long ago. According to Hunt, the Small People are spirits who were not allowed to inherit 'the joys of heaven', (because they lived pre-Christ) but were too good to be condemned to the 'eternal fires'. They diminish in size every year, until they are the size of 'muryans' (ants), at which point they disappear entirely.

Mostly peaceful, they are found all over Cornwall, especially between Penzance and St Just. They can sometimes be benevolent, especially when they discover oppressed poverty. Their help is given freely but, if their assistance is gloated about or shared unfairly, they become angry and their help is taken away. They are wary of humans and withdraw when they sense we are near.

Jack O'Lantern/Jacky Lantern

West Country name for Will-o'-the-Wisp. Jack is a lantern-bearing Fairy who lures unwary travellers astray. He appears as a disembodied flame, sometimes known as a Spunky or Piskey. In some places, he is Pixie King.

Joan the Wad

Queen of the Cornish Piskies, 'Wad' meaning torch/bundle of straw. Joan is often depicted naked. She has a very mischievous nature, but is best known as a good luck charm, bringing health, wealth and happiness to anyone who carries her image. 'Good fortune will nod, if you carry upon you Joan the Wad.'

Spunkies

The Spunkies are believed to be the souls of unbaptised children who act as psychopomps, leading the ghosts of the dead to their final passing place. Spunkies are said to wander the land until Judgement Day (Tongue, 1964, p.94).

Corpse Candles

Corpse candles are spectral light that come with a forewarning of death.

Ruth Tongue records a Somerset woman who saw a floating light move towards a sick woman's cottage door. An hour later she was dead. (Tongue, 1964, p.93)

Derricks

Described as dwarfish spirits of 'somewhat evil nature' in Devon (Wright, 1914, p.206).

They have a better reputation in Hampshire, where they might help locate a lost traveller. Their traditional tales are hard to find, but depicted best in modern Fairy story 'The Derrick' by John Kruse.

Collepixie/Colt Pixey

Thought to be separate from the Pixie family, but sharing their name, the Collepixie is also a trickster, known in and around the New Forest, Hampshire. It is said to take the form of a pony to lure other ponies and travellers deep into the marshy bog to the barrow known as 'Cold Pixie Cave'.

Across the New Forest, the name of the Colt Pixey is interchangeable with Puck and Pooka. This is evident in local place names: Pixey Mead, Picksmoor and Puck Piece. The oldest written reference to any kind of Pixie is Collepixie, featured in Nicholas Udall's translation of *Apophthegmes*:

'I shall be ready at your elbow to play the part of a hobgoblin or collepixie and make thee fear the devil is at your head.' (*Apophthegmes*, 1542).

THE PIXIE COLLECTORS

Anna Eliza Bray (1790–1883)
Collected tales from Dartmoor

Anna Eliza Bray is a key character in the story of the Pixies. Through her writing the Pixies became identified in their own right among British Fairylore.

Bray was a prolific writer and best-selling author during the Victorian period. While in Tavistock, Devon, she published various historical novels and wrote extensive letters describing the history and customs of the town to then poet laureate Robert Southey. The letters, which contained Pixie stories she heard from maidservant Mary Colling, were published in three volumes in 1836: *Traditions, Legends, and Superstitions of Devonshire.*

Bray's books were popular and sold well. The tales of the Pixies caught the imagination of the dawning Victorian era. It is important to note that Bray was influenced by Fairies in wider British literature (Drayton, Shakespeare, Fosbroke, Jonson), which informed her depiction of the Pixies.

Bray received more and more interest in the Pixies, which encouraged her to author a volume of stories inspired by their folklore, *Peep at the Pixies* (1854). Bray's cousin, Christina Rossetti, was inspired by this collection to write her incredible poem 'Goblin Market' in 1859.

Mary Maria Colling (1804–53)
Collected tales from Dartmoor

Mary Maria Colling was the maid servant who told Bray the Pixie stories that were included in her popular work. Colling was a poet and showed her work to Bray who, with Southey, helped Colling publish her work in *Fables and Other Pieces in Verse* (1831). Bray wrote a lengthy introduction to Colling's poetry book, making the class difference between them ever evident. Without Colling, an important part of the Pixies story would never have happened.

Robert Hunt (1807–87)
Collected tales from Cornwall, particularly West Penwith

Robert Hunt was a mineralogist who lectured in mechanical science and contributed a great deal to British mining. He was also an early photographer and antiquarian and passionate about folklore.

Hunt's collection *Popular Romances of the West of England* (1865) was very well received and remains a key text for historical sources on Cornish folklore. Hunt collected some of the tales in his book but had informants across the county who supplied him with content. He acknowledges his two key sources as Thomas Quiller-Couch and William Bottrell.

Hunt was clear that the Cornish Piskey was different from Bray's depiction of a Devon Pixie, which he called a 'harmless creation … rollicking life amidst the luxuriant scenes …' Cornish Piskies, on the other hand, had 'their wits sharpened by their necessities' (Hunt, 1865, p.80).

He was a passionate advocate for the taxonomy of Fairies and identified five types of Spirits in Cornwall: 1. The Small People, 2. Spriggans, 3. Piskies, or Pigsies, 4. Bucca, Bockles or Knockers, 5. Browneys. Unfortunately, Hunt gives just a brief reference to the Browney in the South West, and as this is the only reference they do not feature further in this book.

William Bottrell (1816–81)
Collected tales from Cornwall, particularly West Penwith

William Bottrell was born at Raftra, near Land's End. His father was William Vingoe Bottrell and his mother was Margaret Bosence. (Vingoe, Bottrell and Bosence are all names you will find through his recorded tales). His family, particularly his 'Grandmother Mary', shared many stories with him from an early age, which he worked into his written stories later in life.

Bottrell married, travelled and worked abroad, but returned to Cornwall a poor widower. He lived in a shack on some land at Hawke's point, Lelant, with a black cat called Spriggans, a cow and a pony.

He shared up to fifty stories with Robert Hunt, who published them in his *Popular Romances* in 1865. Encouraged to publish his own, Bottrell spent the last years of his life writing up stories, referring to himself as 'The Old Celt'. Bottrell published articles in periodicals and two volumes of his bestseller *Traditions and Hearthside Stories of West Cornwall* in 1870. He was working on a third when he died, and this was later published with help of Rev. W.S. Lach-Szyrma.

William Crossing (1847–1928)
Collected tales from Dartmoor

Crossing was a leading authority on Dartmoor and its antiquities. Born in Plymouth, he started exploring Dartmoor from an early age. He was a dauntless walker, relentlessly exploring the moor in all weathers. He was passionate about preserving its history and helped re-erect many of the ancient stone crosses that were being used as gateposts.

Importantly for us, Crossing collected and published *Tales of the Dartmoor Pixies* in 1890 while he was living in South Brent. He was well liked and respected by the folk across Dartmoor. He saw great value in their tales and the amount he collected perhaps reflects their confidence in him too. The book remains an invaluable record of Pixie folklore from Dartmoor.

Crossing is best known for his 1909 *Guide to Dartmoor*, which contained extensive and detailed descriptions of Dartmoor's landscape. He and his wife struggled to survive on their modest income and Crossing's health was affected by chronic rheumatism in his later years.

Jonathan Couch (1789–1870), Thomas Quiller-Couch (1826–84), Sir Arthur Thomas Quiller-Couch (1863–1944)
Collected tales from Polperro, Cornwall

Jonathan Couch was born in Polperro and after studying medicine returned to the village to take the position of local doctor. He was a great naturalist with wide-ranging interests. Perhaps naturally for someone who lived in a fishing village, he was interested in fish. Local fishermen brought him specimens from the water, which he studied and painted meticulously. His magnum opus, *History of the Fishes of the British Isles*, was completed in four volumes in 1865. A species of goby fish, *Gobius couchi* (Couch's goby), was named after him.

During his lifetime Couch collected the customs and antiquities of the people of Polperro, including a range of historically important Fairy mythology. He compiled and collected his research into *The History of Polperro*, which remained a manuscript on his death in 1870.

His son, Thomas Quiller-Couch, edited and added to the manuscript, publishing it in 1871. Quiller-Couch was also a doctor, folklorist and writer. He wrote repeatedly for *Notes and Queries* and the *Journal of the Royal Institution of Cornwall*, and importantly was one of the key contributors of folklore and stories to Robert Hunt. Thomas's son, Arthur, became a prolific writer and literary critic himself, sometimes publishing under the pseudonym Q. All three members of this extraordinary family have influenced the pages of this book.

Nellie Sloggett/Enys Tregarthen (1850–1923)
Collected tales around Padstow

Nellie Sloggett was native to Padstow where she spent her whole life. When she was 16, she suffered an illness that left her paralysed. Bedridden for the rest of her life, Sloggett found freedom in stories, books and writing.

During her lifetime she became a prolific writer and published at least eighteen books, at first under Nellie Cornwall and later as Enys Tregarthen. She published *The Piskey-Purse* (1905) and *North Cornwall Fairies and Legends* (1906), both containing authored stories heavily inspired by Cornish folklore and traditional motifs. Because there were very few collectors of folklore on Cornwall's north coast, her work provides an invaluable resource.

Sloggett wrote many characterful tales of the Pixies, always containing sparkling descriptions of the landscape. American writer Elizabeth Yates befriended Sloggett towards the end of her life and collected many of her Pixie tales into *Pixie Folklore and Legends*, published posthumously in 1940.

Ruth Lyndon Tongue (1898–1981)
Collected tales from Somerset

Ruth Tongue was a storyteller, writer and collector of folklore. She was a magical character and an important collector of Pixie stories, particularly from Somerset.

Born to a middle-class family, Tongue spent some of her early childhood in Taunton before returning to Somerset later in life. She was a natural storyteller and her contribution to British folklore remains extensive.

She developed a keen friendship with Katherine Briggs, one of the most influential British folklorists. Tongue shared many stories, quotes and folklore that Briggs included in her collections. Together they published *Folktales of England* in 1965.

Today, Tongue is a controversial figure in folklore. She suffered multiple house fires and lost many of her written records. She depended on her memory for a lot of her work. Many academics have called into question the reliability of her sources and authenticity of her narrative. Her stories have her own enchanting and colourful style. The debate remains how much she embellished and embroidered or fabricated tales that she called traditional.

1

THE VEIL THINS: MEETING THE PIXIES

To meet the Pixies, we must step into the landscape of Cornwall, Devon and Somerset and meet the ancient stories that have defined it: the dance of water and stone.

Somerset has some of the oldest-known rocks in England, dating back around 440 million years ago to the Silurian period. This was a key time in the earth's history, when plants, fungi and arthropods were diversifying and establishing life on its surface.

Around 400 million years ago, the Devonian period followed, covering areas of the South West in a vast shallow sea with coral reefs and volcanic activity. The sandstone, mudstone, limestone and shale we walk on today are remnants from this time. Some 120 million years later, much of the mudstone was baked into slate and thrust into the sky in a period of mountain building. A giant body of subterranean magma intruded beneath the ground, from a colossal chamber called the Cornelian batholith.

Over millions of years, the Cornelian batholith cooled into a great body of granite, stretching over Devon, Cornwall and beyond the Isles of Scilly. The intrusion left the area rich in minerals, particularly cassiterite, copper, lead and china clay. Millions of years and multiple ice ages later, the mountains were weathered away, finally revealing the granite body that continues to define much of the landscape we encounter today.

Around 11,700 years ago, the most recent Ice Age began to retreat. Sea levels rose as the climate defrosted. The region was then shaped by Britain's temperate climate.

This was the landscape that our early ancestors explored, first as moving tribes, then settling, erecting stone monuments, in circles, rows, menhirs and field boundaries. Some of these ancient remnants are funerary sites, others are mysteries. Over the past 4,000 years, miners have sought the rich materials the area has to offer. Home to Celtic Britons, the landscape became known as Dumnonia. The region became smaller and smaller as the Saxons encroached. The ancient people were pushed further and further west. Is this why West Penwith remains filled with stories?

As the Industrial Revolution pulled more people toward cities, stories changed and many stopped being shared. Some tales were recorded in the nineteenth century by enthusiastic folklorists. Coloured by their own intention and bias, these folklorists recorded the traditional tales of the country folk, preserving them in the pages of history.

MODILLA AND PODILLA

Dartmoor, Devon

Our journey into Pixieland begins in South Brent, Devon. Located in the wettest, southern edge of Dartmoor, the moorland village is nestled between the River Avon and the slopes of Brent Hill. The village was mentioned in Domesday Book of 1066, but the prehistoric enclosure of Ryder's Rings at Shipley Bridge show people have called Brent home since the Bronze Age.

Today the village has a vibrant community, environmentally concerned and active in sustainable futures. I grew up in Brent, and am still fascinated by the magical pathways around the village that lead you out on to the open moor.

Our first story was collected by William Crossing, who lived in Brent while he collected and compiled Tales of the Dartmoor Pixies *(1890). This was one of the first stories that introduced me to the enchantment of the Pixies, so it feels fitting that this is where we begin our adventure.*

A long time ago, before my time but not lost to time, there was an old lady who lived in the village of Brent.

She didn't have any children or grandchildren, but everyone called her Grandma Partridge. She was a real local character and held in high regard by all, which is why the village referred to her so affectionately.

Grandma Partridge seemed to enchant every conversation or chore into something special. Her cottage garden was filled with colour, and the children of the village would even call round after school to see if she needed any help.

They would put out or bring in her washing or even weed between her flower beds, because once Grandmother Partridge got talking, magic was never far away.

She had curious names for the flowers. She called the honesty flower 'money-in-both-pockets' – You'll see why when they try to seed!

Purple fuchsias she called 'ladies' eardrops' and the wood sorrel at the gate was always 'cuckoo's bread'. She told the children to take care with the stitchwort. 'Don't pull up any of that! That's the Pixies' favourite flower.'

When they were done, they would put the waste on the compost pile. 'Keep an eye out,' she would say. 'There's a dragon in there!'

And sure enough, on the luckiest days, the children would glimpse a lazy slow worm basking atop the warm pile.

One sunny day in June, Grandma Partridge poured some tea for her little helpers and they asked her for a story.

'What names do the Pixies call each other?' one child asked.

Grandma Partridge's eyes sparkled.

'Well, I don't know if it was their names, or what it was, but this is what happened the first and only time I ever saw the Pixies …

'I must have been about your age,' began Grandma Partridge. 'I was just a girl when my family farmed on the edge of Brent …'

It was a freezing winter, the ground was hard as ice, and the trees all dusted with white. A young Grandma Partridge was working in the kitchen with her mother and sister. Meanwhile, her father was in the fields, mending the old stone walls. Now this day was special – it was her father's birthday – so whilst he toiled away, the three women were secretly making ready a surprise feast!

The family had been on rations since Christmas, so the feast was exciting for all! A joint of meat had been held back for the occasion and was turning on the spit by the fire. The fat was beginning to bubble and burst and the room was filling with the most delicious smell.

Her mother was making a ginger cake (Father's favourite) and a punch for the celebration. The sisters were busy peeling potatoes, carrots and parsnips.

The three of them poured love into what they were doing, and as they worked, fell into a meditative silence.

'That's when it began!' said Grandma Partridge with glee in her voice and sparkle in her eyes.

At that moment, the door came off the latch and opened, just an inch. They felt the January breeze blow in, and all turned, expecting to see the dog at the door…

Each of them was amazed, for in the crack of the door stood the tiny figure of a Pixie.

None of them had ever seen a Pixie before, but you don't mistake it when you see one!

The little being was about eight inches off the ground, dressed in a fine green jacket and skintight trousers, the colour of the first hawthorn leaves in spring. It had roots for shoes and a little red cap on its head.

Each of them froze, as the Pixie skipped its way towards the hearth.

The Pixie paused and regarded the meat on the spit. It was very curious and spent a while inspecting the joint. It must have been satisfied, because it gave a little nod.

Ducking beneath the meat, the Pixie drew close to the fire. It gazed into the flames, transfixed, when suddenly, it plucked a hair from its head and flicked it into the fire.

The three women were entranced and watched as it pulled another hair from its head before flicking it into the blaze.

A third hair was plucked, flicked and floated down into the consuming fire. Just as it was about to pull a fourth hair, a tiny voice called from outside in alarm, 'Modilla! Modilla!'

The Pixie at the fire was startled, suddenly alert.

'Podilla! Podilla!' They cried back.

'Modilla!' urgently repeated the voice outside.

'Podilla!' called the Pixie, and darted, quicker than the wind, across the kitchen and out of the door, which closed shut behind them with a bang!

The three women got up to follow the Pixie. They opened the door to see where it had gone, but the outer door was bolted shut.

The three of them came back into the kitchen when the door burst open behind them. They all jumped in shock! It was Father, in from the fields!

'Did you see the Pixie?' the three of them said together, eyes wide with wonder. He thought they were playing games with him, 'Come off it! Have I caught you red-handed making me a birthday surprise?'

'No, Father, well … yes, Father, but, I promise, it was a real Pixie!'

He looked at them, as his wife tried to hide the cake bowl. 'You've been on the punch already!' he said.

'Father didn't believe at first,' Grandma Partridge said to the children, as she finished her story. 'But something happened over those next weeks.

'We didn't stop talking about the Pixies. We asked the neighbours for their stories and they told us tales even Mother and Father hadn't heard before!

'We started exploring more. Mother taught us the names of the trees and we learnt the medicinal uses of the plants in the hedgerow.

'Father was a thoughtful man and watched the transformation of our family. Even though he never saw them himself, he would always say, he knew the magic of the Pixies after that.'

BATTLE OF PIXIES AND FAIRIES

Blackdown Hills, Somerset

Too much silly discussion regarding the difference between a Fairy and a Pixie. The best way to get to know someone is to meet them, and after that, fight them.

Scuffle and skirmish. Grab a sharp blade of grass! Make it serious.

Must we be at war so early in the book?

Peace, like magic and power, is a difficult thing to hold.

Buckland St Mary is a quiet and peaceful Somerset village. The church stands in the heart of the community opposite the school. You might imagine for a moment there is no calmer place in England. That is what I thought when I visited, until the school bell rang for break time. I was silently reading gravestones when suddenly I was surrounded by the cries and screams of little ones, hidden from sight behind the hedge. The air was electric.

The sudden transformation felt wildly appropriate, seeing as this quiet village is famous for an ancient battle ... Bray and Tongue both tell this story, but my favourite version is told by Owen Staton in his podcast 'Time between Times Storytelling'. This is how the story goes.

Our story begins on Punkie night, the last Thursday in October.* It was autumn and the hedgerows were rich with their treasures of the year. King Oberon, Puck and his royal consort of Fairies showed up to Jack O'Lantern's Pixie ring. Jack O'Lantern and Joan the Wad and a whole host of Pixies welcomed their Fairy cousins and together they revelled.

Of course, the Fairies dressed in red, and the Pixies all in green, so you could tell who was who. I imagine it started with a throwaway comment from Oberon, saying something like, 'Your green outfits really do make you blend in with those weeds.'

Perhaps the Pixies were over-protective; perhaps they were provoked. However it started, a blade was drawn and King Oberon led an angry battalion of Fairies to clash with the Pixies.

The Pixies held a fierce defence. They slipped in and out of visibility; they did indeed blend into the plants rather well. But Fairies are endlessly dangerous and Oberon was certain he would take the victory.

'The South West will be ours!' Oberon called, voice filled with glee, but Jack O'Lantern surprised him with the quickness of his blade, and it flashed Oberon's leg.

'Tis but a scratch,' he called out, but he looked at the wound and all his strength seemed to drain away. The cut turned blue.

Beside himself with fury, Oberon had to pull back. Retreating with his Fairies, he took refuge on the east side of the River Parrett. Oberon sent Puck to fetch him a healing herb that would cure the wound, but from what I've heard, Puck continues to look for it to this day.

From that day to this, the land west of the River Parrett became known as Pixieland and is held by the Pixies still.

---

* *Punkie night is a seasonal celebration in Somerset, where local children go begging for candles, to light up hollowed turnips, mangolds or pumpkins.*

NANNY NORRISH

Dartmoor, Devon

> I shall by some be thought to lead you in a Pixy-path by telling an old tale.
>
> Thomas Westcote, *c.*1630

Many moons ago, there was an old schoolmaster in Widdecombe called John Norrish. He was disabled, but that did not stop him giving generously to the children on the moor. Unfortunately for the children of Widdecombe, he was not a very learned man and his lessons were rather less than 'planned'. But he didn't charge the parents much for the service. He believed that everyone should be entitled to an education. He was known as 'Honest John'.

So honest was he that he barely made enough money to support his wife, Nanny. However, she loved that John's kindness was a lesson the children learned early in life. Besides, together with her work as a washerwoman, they got by.

Nanny would walk long and far to farms and houses across the moor who employed her to do their washing, and she wouldn't leave 'til everything had been washed and mangled and hung up to dry on the gorse bushes.

She was a good-natured soul, and always had warmth to share. She would stay for dinner if she had worked later than usual, even though her employers would say, 'It will be late for your journey home. Don't you mind the Pisgies?'

She would laugh off their superstitious beliefs, saying, 'Come now! The Pisgies are a lovely story, best kept for grannies. I'm not that old yet, thank you very much.'

She walked home muttering to herself, 'Pisgies indeed! I can't believe people are so easy to believe what they cannot see! If I did meet one, I'm sure I wouldn't be afraid.'

She continued on her way, laughing at the idea.

That night she was home late and John was in a rotten mood after a day of teaching 'unruly children' as he grumbled. 'I thought you had met with the Pixies for sure tonight,' he said.

'Come on, John, not you as well!' It's wild how many people are so gullible to the old stories. If this is the sort of stuff you're teaching your children then little wonder they are unruly.'

One evening in darkest winter, Nanny had been working at Dockwell Farm. It was dark so early that the stars were already in the sky when she finished work.

The people of the house lit a lantern for her journey home, bidding her be careful not to be led away by the Pixies.

'Oh drat the Pisgies!' exclaimed Nanny, as she tied up her bonnet strings. 'I don't believe there's wan left! Of course, people have said they have seen 'em, but I can't believe it, not 'til I've seen one myself. But I hardly think that's likely.' She was quite a force when riled. 'Goodnight!' she said and she walked away, leaving the lantern behind.

Up the lane she went, past Hut Holes, and up towards Wind Tor. She could see by the position of the stars that even though the time was getting on, it was earlier than she had promised to be home, so she was pleased with herself. The walking soothed her, and she soon forgot all about her annoyance and the Pixies.

But the Pixies had not forgotten Nanny. Their long ears had heard her words, they had felt her feelings, and they always regarded her with amusement … until tonight.

'She thinks we've died out?' said a Pixie.

'"A lovely story, best kept for grannies," is what she said.'

'If I did meet one I'm sure I wouldn't be afraid!' added another, imitating her.

'"Drat the Pisgies" indeed! Well, well, well,' said another, grinning ear to ear. 'Nanny Norrish, it might just be high time to make you more careful of your words.'

The quartet of Pixies disappeared into the darkness like ink into a midnight sea.

Nanny Norrish trudged on, up the hill, planning out her work schedule for the next day. She thought about dinner and remembered all of her own washing that she hadn't quite managed to fit in before work, when suddenly …

Voices spoke around her. As if nonsense words were falling out of the sky, she turned to seek where they were coming from, but they were everywhere. The words made no sense, until she realised they were her own words echoed back to her.

Nanny stopped walking to collect her senses. All fell silent. Suddenly the moon arose behind her, shining a bright light upon her path, illuminating the most extraordinary sight.

She saw before her a huge crowd of the smallest folk, standing on one another's shoulders, forming a living pyramid. A tower of bodies kept growing and growing, swaying and swaying until a veritable Tower of Babel swung about the Dartmoor skyline, taller than any tor, a giant body made up of so many parts.

Nanny stood in awe, looked up at the swaying tower, and had the biggest smile on her face. 'What a way to be proven wrong,' she whispered to herself.

A cloud passed over the moon, the Pixies were gone with a laugh.

Nanny told her story to amazed faces, and told all who would listen how she had been wrong about the spirits.

'Oh I stand utterly corrected,' she would always say, 'apart from one thing … A wonder like what I saw, I knew I didn't need be afraid.'

THE BROKEN PED

Wick Moor, Somerset

Wick Moor can be found north of Bridgewater, along Somerset's coastline. In a spot looking out towards the Bristol Channel lay the remains of a Bronze Age burial chamber known as Pixies Mound. The tumulus was excavated in 1907, revealing human remains and Beaker-ware pottery that date the mound to around 1800 BC. A brass Roman coin was found alongside, indicating that the Romans had visited around AD 336, offering a coin in exchange for any pilfered riches.

The fields around the mound were called Pixypiece and stories still linger of enchanted happenings. Stephen Dewar records that this is one of many sites where 'unearthly music rises from the ground' (Brown & Dewar, 1968, p.10).

In November 1957 construction began on the £70 million atomic power station at Hinkley Point, Stogursey, absorbing the mound within its fences. The completion of the project was significantly delayed, resulting in the Central Electricity Generating Board reporting in their opening brochure that the delays were down to the mischievous interference of the Pixies (Hurley, 1973).

In widespread Fairy lore stretching all the way back to the Greek tale of Persephone, eating food from the other world results in death or eternal captivity. The following story (similar to The Ploughman's Breakfast*, Crossing, 1890) is an example of Pixy food being offered as a blessing.*

One morning, a farm labourer who had just become a new father was walking across Wick Moor. He heard the sound of a child crying and immediately his gut wrenched, thinking of his own babe. He looked around but no one could be seen. Instinctively he knew these were not the cries of a human child.

In a few steps, he came across a child's ped (spade/shovel) broken in half.

He picked it up and it didn't take long before he restored it to new.

He put it on a raised mound of earth. He looked everywhere for the one who had been crying, but there was no one to be found. As he left, he called out loud, 'There it is then. Cry no more.'

On his return home from work, he passed the mound again and had a look. The ped was gone but the smallest, freshest, finest, baked cake lay in its place.

'No way you're gunna eat that?' said his companion in warning, 'Don't you know this is Pixies Mound?'

To his friend's horror, he ate it and 'proper good' it was too.

'Goodnight to 'ee,' he called out as he went.

His companion expected him to drop dead at any moment. He prospered ever after.

FAIRY FUNERAL

Lelant Towans, Cornwall

Britain's coastal dunes are one of the most threatened habitats in Europe. In Cornwall they are called Towans (meaning sand dunes). They are home to the silver-studded blue butterfly (best seen in June) and rare petalwort, an extraordinarily beautiful type of liverwort.

Folklorist Margaret Ann Courtney (1834–1920) notes how the Towans contain many secrets. The Lelant Towans hide the former residence of King Theodrick, who escaped Ireland after beheading many saints. Buried on the other side of the River Hayle lies the castle of pagan chief Tendar. Courtney also notes that the lost church of Perranzabuloe was thought to have been a myth, until shifting sands in 1835 revealed an oratory and church in Penhale Sands (Courtney, 1890, p.68). My grandfather, born in St Agnes, was christened 'St Piran' in the ruins of this medieval church in 1920!

Perhaps it is no surprise that there are repeated stories of the Piskeys in the Towans. For the next story we must visit St Uny Church set in the sandy hills of Lelant Towans. It is not known how old the church is, but the earliest records go back to 1150. The church outdates the neighbouring church St Ia's in St Ives. It is worth noting that St Ia must have been the most dainty saint, having crossed the waters from Ireland on a leaf (was she a Piskey?). The sands of the Towans are ever moving and by 1538 St Uny was part-buried by the blown sand.

It has been postulated that this story may be a distant memory of an ancient saint buried at St Uny's church.

The moonlight shone off the Towans between Carbis Bay and Godrevy Point. It was about midnight when Richard was returning home from St Ives market. It was fishing season and another record catch of pilchards had been brought into St Ives harbour. They were saying it might be the biggest haul British waters had ever recorded. What a time to be alive! He brought a great bundle of pilchards home with him that night.

There was something about the way the moonlight bounced off the sand that reminded him of a similar evening when he was much younger, when, on this sandy landscape, he had seen into the other world.

Walking through the Towans, he had come across a whole host of Little Folk celebrating a season's feast.

These tiny people surrounded a richly laid table. It was filled with fruits and flowers, honeys and milks, leaves of gold and tin, and vessels of glass, silk and slate filled with jams and cheeses, breads and meats.

He was amazed, but not very discreet. He disturbed them and they vanished.

He was forever known as the man who let gold slip between his fingers after that.

He didn't mind the gold, he was amazed to know that such a wonder was possible to witness. How endlessly abundant this world.

All these years later, he still felt cautious walking across the Towans at night. He knew they would still be there. He turned away from the headland towards the village, past St Uny church, when the muffled mournful dirge of the church bell rang out. A great feeling of unease made Richard turn towards the church, to see who was ringing at such a late hour.

Steadily, the bell continued to toll heavily, with no echo; it filled him with such sorrow. At first he thought it was the moon that illuminated the church so brightly, but no, it was coming from within the church. Such a light, unforgettably bright. It was as if the church held a door open to morning.

As he drew up to the window, he saw movement inside … shapes formed a huge procession of tiny people flooding their way up the central aisle. Small folk, many hundreds of them, handsomely dressed, stretched everywhere, draped over the pews. Wreaths of delicate rambling rose ran between them, and many carried branches of flowering myrtle. Surely they were in some grand celebration … but their movements were slow and sorrowful.

A group of them brought a corpse covered in flowers into the funeral procession. The corpse was heartbreakingly beautiful, her golden hair interwoven with blossoms. Surely it was the most beautiful face he had ever seen, tiny yet so bright. The sorrow he felt was as if an angel had died.

She was taken to the altar, where small folk with picks and spades dug into the floor by the sacramental table and the body was lowered gently.

By now the church was filled with a colossal crowd of Little Folk. They gathered around to glimpse the last sight of her as she was lowered into the earth.

The rose and myrtle branches were thrown into the grave as suddenly a chorus called out 'Our Queen is dead! Our Queen is dead! Our Queen is dead!'

Devotions poured over their Queen, as the crowd of spirits let out a shriek so alarming that Richard involuntarily joined in.

As his voice joined theirs, the light extinguished, the spirits and the grave disappeared and the church was emptied.

Many invisible things brushed past the terrified man, shrieking, piercing him with sharp instruments. He turned and ran home.

2

STRANGE SIGHTS: NEIGHBOURLY RELATIONS

Pixies are said to delight in the solitary places, deep in the hills and in pathless woods. It's easy to understand why when you explore the unparalleled coastline and luminescent light of West Penwith. Walk through the marshy land of Goss Moor in the mist and you will see it. Feel the folds of Dartmoor stretch your legs and you will know it. Taste the treasures of autumn in the Blackdown Hills and it will be obvious! Watch the sun through the trees in the Quantocks and you will be left without doubt … The Pixies choose their homes with utmost taste.

Don't think all this beauty is idyllic! There are many monarchies among Pixies, which dramatically increases the likelihood of war. We have already seen bloody battles in the story 'Battle of Fairies and Pixies' and there will inevitably be more to come.

Their chief delight is said to be dancing, but equally it could be Pixy-leading people astray – they are seen laughing in both activities. We will see repeated examples of all of the above. But it's not all fun and games, Pixies have work to do, and what's worse, the stretches of land they call home have been sought out by humans for years. We have become their neighbours, and they ours.

Are we good neighbours?

Luckily, for much of the South West, many of our Pixie neighbours seem curious about human ways.

They have developed preferences for freshly swept hearths, and are willing to help farmers who are overwhelmed with work or who suffer abject poverty.

Over the next chapter, we will see how relationships with the 'good neighbours' have developed across Pixieland.

Remember! Their eyes ever watch, their ears ever listen. It's best to keep good neighbourly relations.

TWO MOONS IN MAY

Somerset

More often than not, Fairy gold disappears after the sun goes down. Sometimes, as with the next story, the Fairy assists its human neighbour out of gratitude. Don't forget to leave your offerings out for the spirits.

Well water, scalded cream, milk, a clean hearth, and honeycomb are traditional offerings in Somerset.

Way back, there used to be an old couple who lived near Pitminster in Somerset. Old Sammy and Old Nanny worked a small bit of land where they had an acre of hay, an acre of corn and a little bit of garden.

They had a cow and her calf, a pig, two or three hens and a dunk to carry their goods to Taunton market.

They never had much to sell … a few eggs, sometimes a bit of butter, whatever green goodness came out of the garden, berries or apples if it was their season. But they were famous knitters and people always bought their stockings, so they usually had enough to get by.

One May day, Old Sammy comes in saying, 'It's a full moon tonight, and on May first too.'

Old Nanny looks at him with a sharp look, 'Oh … that's bad!' She almost looked out the window to check, but saved herself in time. 'I must be very careful when I look up. It isn't a very lucky time, when *They're* about.' She knew it wasn't wise to name names.

'That means there'll be a second moon this month,' says Old Sammy.

'Two moons in May! We'll be lucky if we get corn or hay.'

He looks at her, but she just says, 'Somehow, we'll get by.'

She was right, the weather was shocking, most of the corn went black and the little that didn't was hung up on the fences to dry. The corn stood in the rain until it sprouted. There were no plums that year and the raspberries all went mouldy. Even the sow only gave birth to five piglets.

'Somehow, we'll get by,' Old Nanny says.

Their stocking money just about kept them, but it didn't save them enough to buy any more wool. Rent day was coming so they sold their Sunday best and still it continued to rain.

The year was grim indeed and they knew more bad weather was coming. They looked at each other and knew they would have to sell the old dunk and the cow and her calf to cover the rent over the winter. If they were lucky, they would have a few shillings left to last them 'til spring.

Nanny sat by the fire and was about to say, 'Somehow, we'll get by,' but the words got stuck in her throat. No cow meant that they would no longer have fresh milk to set out at night for Them. She had kept the old ways, every day of her life. Maybe this time, they wouldn't get by. She sobbed.

Old Sammy walked to the spring for some fresh water. 'They'll know not to blame us,' he thought to himself. While he was walking, he came upon three bags lying on the road. One was blue, full to bursting and chinked. The next was red, about half full. The last was a pretty little green thing, flat empty.

Old Sammy picked up the bags, wondering who had been so unlucky to lose their fortune? Suddenly, a new plan formed in his head. He remembered one last pair of stockings that he had stashed away. And a few apples! So he decided he would take those to market the next day. Maybe they could keep the animals after all. Maybe they really would get by.

Old Nanny stashed the bags in the thatch for safekeeping. She went out to brush the animals and milk the cow one last time. She knew Old Sammy wouldn't be able to make enough money at the market. She would have to give away her animals when the landlord arrived for his rent. The best bit of cream was placed out on the hearth that night, one last time.

When Old Sammy came home from market, he showed her the pennies he had made from selling the apples and the stockings. They both sighed, it wasn't anywhere near enough.

'Oh, I had the Bellman cry for the lost bags … there was plenty who claimed them for their own, but nobody rightly, so I came on home.'

He hadn't stopped talking when there was a knock at the door. There was Old Sal Shack, the black witch.

'Those bags are mine,' she said as soon as the door was open.

'What are the words written on them?' Old Nanny asked, as fast as a swift.

'Harum Scarum!' said Old Sal.

'Out you go,' said Old Sammy and sent her away.

It wasn't too long before there was another knock at the door. An old poacher came to claim the bags.

'What are the words written on them?'

He paused for a moment and said 'Oliver's Dark?' He was sent away too.

The old folks sat down at the fire fearing the morning. There was another knock at the door. This time it was a stranger in green.

'I've come for my bags!' he said, smiling at them.

'What are the words written on them?'

'There are no words written on them, none at all.' Old Nanny felt better at once. They both knew he was the right one.

'I'll be back to collect them tomorrow. We appreciate you putting out cream and going without. Let's see what we can do about the rent in the morning!'

They were stunned!

Early next morning the stranger in green stood outside the gate, smiling at them. 'You better take that dunk away from here to graze. We don't want her spoiling my plan! Give me the three bags and don't come back here till the sun has set over the elm treetop!'

He smiled and they left him with the three bags. The stranger in green sat on a bench outside the farm, with the three bags in a row beside him.

The landlord rode up to the house on a rattail pony. 'I've come for my rent.'

The stranger in green pointed to the fat blue bag that chinked. 'There is enough in that bag to cover the rent and buy the farm outright,' he says.

The landlord counted all the gold and discovered far more in the bag than the tiny farm was worth.

'Erm, yes … yes. That seems about right.' The landlord smiled, and suddenly in a hurry, gave a receipt to the green man for the sale of the farm, and scarpered away with the cash.

Just as he disappeared, the parson came along on a fine cob. 'This property owes me my tithes,' he said and the green stranger gave him the coins in the red bag. Off the parson went.

The green stranger watched as the sun started to set in the Elm treetop. The old couple returned with their dunk, and the green stranger handed them the green bag. 'This bag is for you. The others have been claimed. You now own the farm. Don't forget the cream tonight.' In the fading light he seemed to disappear down the green lane, just like that.

Old Nanny prepared a fresh bowl of cream and said to Old Sammy, 'It would be a shame, but we could sell the green bag, it's so pretty.'

The next morning they felt the green bag and there was a bit of money in the lining. It was a whole golden guinea.

They bought something to eat and had a good fire that night. When they looked the next day, there was another guinea in the lining.

It was the same the next day and the next … the bag was never empty after that.

Old Sammy heard that the landlord was seen in a blind rage when he later opened the blue bag to find it full of yellow moss. On Sunday morning the congregation watched amazed as the parson's coat-tails caught on fire when he walked up the aisle. They pulled his flaming cassock off him and discovered a charred red bag beneath.

The weather improved that week and Old Sammy and Old Nanny got by very well after that.

TWO PIXIE THRESHERS

Devon

'There's thresh going on everywhere,' said Chaffy Grain, who then disappeared.

Once upon a time, curious things happened to an old woman in Tavistock. She would come downstairs to see much of her flax had been spun in the night. One evening she came downstairs and spied a little raggedy creature, who jumped out the door as soon as it saw her.

A Pixie! It had been spinning her flax. The feeling of gratitude she felt was so great! She decided to send her thanks. So she bought some doll clothes (pretty little things they were) and placed them by her spinning wheel.

When the Pixie returned and put on the clothes, it clapped its tiny hands and was heard to exclaim:

Pixie fine, Pixie gay!
Pixie now will run away!

And off it went! That old woman never saw the Pixie again.

Once upon another time, there was a farmer whose barn was visited by a whole troop of Pixies. Under cover of darkness they would thrash wheat for him for nothing but their own amusement. The farmer couldn't help but look and caught sight of the whole troop hard at work with his flails.

'Niver did I see such drashers as they was.'

He watched until eventually one said to the other, 'I twit [sweat], don't you twit?'

He must have made a sound because suddenly they were alert. They all ran away except for one little one who stumbled and fell. The farmer ran in and caught him and put him into his lantern, where he lived for some time. One night the farmer lifted the lantern and the lock came loose. He tried to close it but the Pixie was quicker. It jumped out saying, 'Here I goes, here I goes.'

The farmer never saw him again.

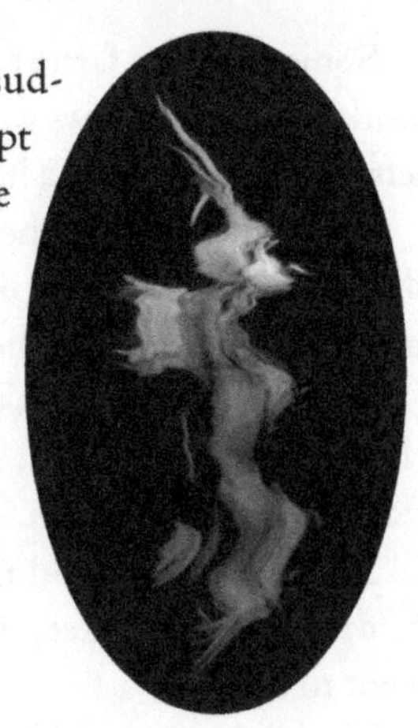

WITHYPOOL DINGDONGS

Exmoor, Somerset

The village of Withypool is located along the River Barle in the hills of Exmoor. The Anglican church of St Andrew's dates back to the late medieval times, perhaps the memory of this tale dates back to those days? Ruth Tongue recorded it in 1965, but the earliest version I have found is in Frederick John Snell's Book of Exmoor *(1903).*

Across Somerset, it was wise to leave the last apples on the trees for the Pixy folk. 'Pixie-hoard' or 'Pixy word' (Palmer, 1976) were the names given to the offerings left on the trees after the orchards have been picked.

It makes sense then, that 'to Pixy' (in West Somerset) or to go 'Pixy-wording' (Wright, 1914) is to glean stray apples in an orchard after the trees have been stripped.

The King of the Pixies lived at Knighton Farm in the Withypool Parish on Exmoor. Long and happy did the Pixies live alongside their human neighbours.

Sometimes the farmer didn't have enough people to help with his workload, so the Pixies would come into his barn and thresh the corn left unprocessed after a hard day's work.

One summer, when the family were especially struggling, the Pixies did an immense amount of work. The farmer's grateful wife could not resist peeping through the keyhole to finally see them.

They were strange, naked, hairy little things. She wasn't afraid of their squinting eyes, but she did feel sorry that they only had their body hair to keep warm.

She set to work and made some tiny outfits she judged would fit them nicely and keep them warm. She left them in the barn and went to bed.

Maybe they were offended, maybe they were thrilled; whatever it was, they never came back to help after that.

The family prospered, but lived in regret after the Pixies disappeared. The farmer and his wife wondered if they might come back or if they had left the area entirely. Times were changing and Withypool village grew and got itself a brand new church. The farmer felt his wife's sorrow and always told her when he saw fresh gallitraps (Pixy rings) in the fields. Whenever they walked in the woods, they noticed there was still *that* feeling. They always made sure to leave the 'Pixies-hoard' on the trees.

One day, to the farmer's great surprise, the Pixie King walked up to meet him, in an upland field.

'Wilt gie us the lend of thy oss an crooks?' spoke the Pixie.

The farmer looked at his little neighbour cautiously. He knew the Pixies liked riding ponies ragged.

'What vor?' The farmer eyed him cautiously.

'I d'want to take my good wife an littlings out of the noise of they ding-dongs.'

The farmer set the crooks on the back of his horses and trusted them to the Pixies.

So it was that the Pixies left Knighton Farm. They loaded those packhorses full and moved lock stock and barrel to Winsford Hill. When the old pack horses trotted home, they had been changed to beautiful two-year-olds.

COLMAN GREY

Polperro, Cornwall

Colman Grey appears among the rich Fairy mythology of Polperro, collected by Jonathan Couch (1789–1870). This story seems a popular tale, a similar version appears in West Penwith titled 'A Fairy Caught'/'Skillywidden' (Hunt, 1865). William Percy Merrick also recorded a version from Ottery St Mary in 1911.

'Laugh like a Piskey' was a popular saying.

The farmer turned to head home. The weather was heavy above him; it didn't look like he was going to get home before the rain.

A large stone caught his eye. Was that a bird sitting there? It almost looked like a tiny figure … A doll perhaps?

He drew closer and realised to his amazement it was a tiny little fellow.

One of the Good Folk! A real Elvish man.

The little man turned and caught the farmer's eye. He was sad, cold and miserable. The farmer felt overwhelmed with pity.

'You look cold and hungry. I'm on my way home, do you need some warming up?' The farmer put out his hand, knowing the best way to treat the Good Folk is with best generosity.

The little one jumped up on to his shoulder, lighter than a bird. The farmer's smile had never felt bigger as he made his way back home that day. He hardly felt the rain.

His wife watched, amazed as her husband and the Piskey came into the kitchen that evening. Her husband headed toward the fire, where the little figure jumped down and investigated the hearth. The farmer's wife brought some milk and cheese and a cloth so he could dry himself.

The Piskey was much happier after a bit of food and some time by the fire.

It jumped up and started leaping across the room from table to shelf, cup to candle.

The husband and wife both found the visitor very welcome and they laughed as the little figure somersaulted along the leeks. onto the cabbages and across the kitchen surfaces, landing with a splash in the sink.

They tried to encourage the wee fellow to talk. They repeatedly spoke their names, but the little figure just cocked its head as if it were a robin.

Over the coming days the Piskey brought such energy into the house, it was as if the farm were full of children again. It was as curious as a kitten about all things in the farmhouse. It found the spoons fascinating, and for reasons unknown to the farmer's wife, it seemed to think that anything coming out of the oven – whether pot, pan or pie – was the perfect place to dance.

The joy in the house was cut short suddenly when a voice was heard outside calling, 'Colman Grey! Colman Grey! Colman Grey!'

The Piskey jumped up and surprised them all by saying, 'Ho! Ho! Ho! My Daddy is come!'

It leapt into the air, shot like a bullet, and disappeared out of the keyhole, never to be seen again.

The farmer and his wife missed their little visitor, but a little of the energy he had brought stayed with them, and the rest of their days were brighter for it.

DEAL WITH THE KNOCKERS

West Penwith, Cornwall

In the dripping depths of Cornwall's roots, Knockers follow the richest paths of minerals in the granite. They are also referred to as Bucca, Gathorns, Nickers, Nuggies or Imps – if they're naughty. If they allow themselves to be seen, they appear as diminished men, usually with beards with their own Fairy tools. They worked hard in the mines, knocking at the metals in the rock for their own interests. Oftentimes they could be found imitating their human companions, as we will see in later stories.

At Ransom Mine in the far reaches of Cornwall, it is said that the Knockers worked hard and long. They communicated with the human miners by knocking on the lode. If a steady knocking was heard, you'd be wise to follow it, for the spirits were leading you to a good stream of tin or copper. If you heard fast knocking, it was a sign to get out of the mine as soon as possible, for a collapse was sure to follow.

Miners didn't always feel brave enough to follow the sounds of the spirits down into the darkness. Some found other ways …

There was one particular part of Ransom Mine where the knocking was continual.

'It's not safe,' people said, 'It's a lure,' others threatened.

But if the Knockers were working continually, it had to be a sign of a massive lode.

An old man called Trenwith had a plan. He had spent his life in the mines and a great deal of time thinking about his subterranean companions. He had left out offerings, given many tributes, and had listened to their knockings, to the stories and all the superstitions.

'Come for a walk with me tonight,' he told his son one midsummer evening. He and his son made their way above ground to the part of the mine that the miners called 'Buckles ground'. In the cracked opening there, the Knockers could be heard from above ground. Here the old man and his son waited.

The son thought his dad must have lost it. To waste the midsummer celebrations hanging out at work! But his father had been adamant. It must have been around midnight when something happened. A small figure rose out of the crack in the ground, bringing some shining ore with it.

Another and another followed, laden with more glorious ore. The old man smiled, his son was flabbergasted.

'It's, it's, it's the Smae People!' his son said stupidly, before his father hushed him.

His father approached the Fairy people and made a comment on the fine lode they had found.

The Knockers were accepting of the company of the old man and took a liking to him. He suggested he could help them in their work.

'If you bring up the ore "to grass" for us, then my son and I could properly dress the metal and leave the richest 10 per cent for you. How does that sound?'

The Knockers liked the deal and an agreement was made.

The father and son took the pitch and in a short time they were seeing a great return for the ore they had to sell. The old man never failed to keep up his bargain – he always left the best of it for the Knockers, and treated them as his friends 'til the ends of his days.

Eventually, the old man passed away, and his son got greedy. He started not leaving the best bits of the lode for the spirits, and then he started leaving less than was rightfully theirs.

The Knockers don't like a cheat – they felt his selfishness and they abandoned him. No longer did they bring up the ore to that green grass, and so the deal failed. Their knocking continued relentlessly, but he never saw a single sparkle of it. Nothing seemed to go right with him after that.

He turned to drink, squandered the money his father saved and died a beggar.

TOM TREVORROW

West Penwith, Cornwall

It is no surprise that in such a dangerous workplace as the copper and tin mines, superstitions were shared and hopes held by those who gave their life to work there.

Miners believed snails in the mine were signs of good luck, but if you spotted a toad in a tunnel it was even better. If you heard a rat squeal, it was a sure sign you should retreat. Above all, it was widespread that you should never whistle or swear down in the mine, for the sprits don't like it.

Miners would leave a bit of food such as fuggan (fruit cake) as an offering to the spirits. Even today there are people who will leave a portion of their pasty for the Piskeys.

Tom Trevorrow had been a miner all his life, and a proud one at that. He had already spent twenty years down in Cornish mines when our story begins. His eldest son, Billy, was still only a boy but he was at the age when he could start working down in the mines. Times were not easy for miners. Work had dried up at his last bal, so Tom looked for new work that he and his boy could do.

They needed more men at Ballowall mine, so the family relocated to St Just, at the very tip of Cornwall's toes.

Tom and his son Billy were sent to work on the Buckshaft, deep in an old part of the mine. They changed their clothes and were introduced to several miners, and it didn't take long for the old boys to mention the spirits. 'The Buckshaft is wild old,' said a friendly chap, looking at the boy. 'This mine was worked on in the days before Noah's flood. It's full of spirits. Careful how you go, don't forget to pay *Them* their dues.'

Tom said nothing but when they were alone he leaned close to his son and said, 'Don't fall prey to the superstitious and gullible. The shadows cast by the candles on our helmets play all sorts of tricks on the mind. It ain't no Piskey that eats up the fuggan these old fools leave … it's mice.'

It was a sprawling old mine. Endless passageways and great dropping shafts cut deep into the land. The tunnels followed veins of lode in the stone, and some of the tunnels even went under the sea. In these tunnels you could hear the tossing tide right above your head.

They journeyed deep into the belly of the mine and were soon at work in the Buckshaft. It wasn't long before they were both sweating away. Billy was slower than his dad, and when he paused he could hear the sound of tools clattering and clanging against the rock.

'What's that noise, Da? Is that the Knockers?'

'That's what they say.'

'What do we do? Should we follow them or get away?'

His dad ignored him and continued striking the stone.

'They don't sound far away … Should we give them some food? Da?'

Tom stayed silent.

When they stopped for lunch, the knocking in the walls continued.

Billy looked at his dad, but didn't repeat his questions. He was amazed to hear the spirits so close, he even heard squeaking sounds … they must be speaking. Secretly he left some food in a hidden spot before returning to work.

After long weeks of hard work, they had started to collect a good pile of ore. It was relentless work and one day, exhausted, Billy stayed at home to rest.

Tom descended into the darkness of the Buckshaft, where the sounds of knocking and hammering met him again, closer than ever. So close that Tom could hear their voices.

They were excited about something, it was a continual chorus of confounding chatter and tee-hee-heeing.

It distracted Tom and he kept slipping as he struck the rock. Every time he missed his aim, he heard laughter in reply.

It happened again and again, and Tom steamed in frustration. They were mocking him.

He struck another clumsy blow and the chorus laughed out at him. He picked up some rocks from his feet and threw them to the wall.

'Go to blazes, you cussed old devil sperrats! I'll scat [knock] your brains out, I will, ef you aren't gone from here.'

No sooner had he said it but stones above his head dislodged and a little shower fell around him.

Frightened out of his senses, he retreated quickly … this was a miner's worst nightmare.

He paused, frozen to the spot, but no more came. He breathed a huge sigh of relief.

All was silent now in the tunnel. He refused to give up, but his candle had burnt down so he replaced it and took a break.

Laying his back against the wall, he opened up his lunch of fuggan.

It was only a sliver, but he savoured it.

A squeaky voice sung out from the wall behind him.

'Tom Trevorrow! Tom Trevorrow! Give Bucca some fuggan or bad luck tomorrow.'

Tom thought he must be going mad, but the voice kept repeating, as he kept eating. There was a fight in him, a kick back, a resilience that kept him hard as nails, the kind of strength a miner needed. He trusted it and he ate the last bit of his fuggan, not persuaded by the voices he heard in his mind. All the fuggan was gone. An unearthly silence filled the mine and not even a drop of water fell.

He waited, but nothing happened.

He got up, brushed his knees and picked up his tools.

The squeaky voice returned, angry now,

Tommy Trevorrow! Tommy Trevorrow!
We'll send thee bad luck tomorrow!
Thou old Curmudgeon, to eat all thy fuggan,
and not leave a didjan for Bucca!

They sang it again and again, louder and louder, 'til Tom was petrified. He walked away until the voices were out of hearing. He felt dizzy. He found a dry spot and sat, taking out his pipe to calm himself. He thought he would close his eyes for a few minutes, but as soon as they were shut, sleep took him.

He woke to the flickering low flame of his new candle about to burn out. He must have slept for hours.

He looked into the darkness and saw eyes surrounding him staring back at him.

Hundreds of terrifying ugly eyes. Miserable, little, old withered creatures, the tallest of them no more than 3ft 6in, or there about, with shanks like drumsticks, and arms as long as their legs. They had big ugly heads, with grey or red locks, squinting eyes, dirty beards and mouths from ear to ear.

One older and uglier than the rest (if that was possible) seemed to smile in a disconcerting way. The creature put a thumb to his nose and squinted at Tom, and suddenly all of those around him did the same. They lolled out their tongues and grinned at Tom, who had never felt so scared in a mine in all his life.

In that moment his candle burnt out on to the clay. He stumbled to get a new candle in the holder but as soon as it was lit the little creatures were gone.

Tom left his tools, left the pile of ore and made for the ladder to get back up to the blacksmith's shop at the top of the mine. It took more energy than he thought possible to climb that ladder. He got back to the shop and sat gasping for air. The other miners there saw the fear still on his face and he told them what had happened.

'How could ee be so foolish as to not leave some fuggan? Tis the custom to leave something on the ground for good luck.'

'No surprise to see such things if you're working in the Buckshaft boy!' said another miner. 'The shaft was named because a black buck-goat, or a Bucca in shape of one, was seen down there, but never found. It's swarming with Knockers down there.'

Tom went home shaky that night, but refused to tell his wife or Billy about what had happened.

The next day Billy and Tom returned to the mine and descended to the Buckshaft.

'Let's pull up the lode we have already collected,' Tom said to his son, trying to hide his feelings of unease.

Billy stayed by the winch at the top of the vertical shaft called a 'winze', while Tom descended to secure the lode.

Tom secured the heavy lode and tied the other end to his waist, while he climbed the ladder to secure the rope to the winch. He had only climbed a few steps up when a frantic knocking started all around him. It was wild and fast, like nothing he had ever heard before, but he knew what it meant.

Instinctively, he untied the rope around his waist and just in time as the ground holding the Buckshaft gave way. The lode and all his tools fell away into impenetrable depths of the mine.

Tom pulled himself back up to safety, but all the work was wasted and his expensive tools were lost. He left the mine, and without tools he was in a pickle. He had no choice but to work on a farm – a great shame for a proud tinner, he thought.

'Since then my bad luck has never ended,' he would say to anyone who listened. Years of bad luck did seem to follow Tom, until eventually, in secret, his wife employed a peddler to work a charm on him. Incredibly, good luck did return. He was free from the wrath of the Knockers. But it did not help him make better decisions in the future.

Billy made a different way. He never forgot the power of the subterranean spirits and always gave them the reverence he felt they deserved. Secretly, he disagreed with his father. The way he saw it, his Da had been blessed by incredible fortune, not bad luck. If he hadn't had time to untie that rope, they would have pulled him to his death.

Billy turned into a fine miner and travelled to the American West to work in mines out there. He had only been underground a day or two when he heard it. He told the tales he knew so well, and the American miners gave them the name Tommyknockers. People said Billy brought the spirits with him when he emigrated to the New World.

Folk tales and poems of the Tommyknockers can still be found in America.

3

WHEN THE FEN RISES: PIXY-LED

'Belated', 'benighted', 'bewildered', 'maze' and 'mystified.'

If you have been disorientated and unaccountably lost, particularly in a familiar landscape, it's likely you have been Pixy-led. It is widely believed, particularly across the moors of the South West, that the Pixies control the mist, so, take care if you suddenly find yourself surrounded by fog! Day or night, confused victims are repeatedly dumbfounded and met with laughter and clapping – aha! Pixies are about.

Accounts dating from mid-sixteenth century to the present day continue to report 'Pixy-led' misadventures. It could be Jack O'Lantern himself, King of the Pixies. Or, if you are in Cornwall, perhaps it's Joan the Wad, Queen of the Piskies? Both are local names for the wandering flame, better known as Will-o'-the-Wisp.

Baring-Gould recorded that the best time to see Jack O'Lantern is during a hot summer, between July and September. This is, as the moormen say, 'When the 'vaen' (fen) rises', i.e. when there is fermentation going on in the marsh/fen.

One Cornish doctor suggested that 'Piskey-led is often whiskey led'. Of course, a lot of these occurrences could be explained by atmospheric conditions, darkness, intoxicants or simple confusion etc., but it is curious that the phenomenon is concentrated to particular areas. Perhaps having the language available to describe it enables better awareness of it?

Regional accounts of being lost might sound trivial, but perhaps there is something potentially profound in the concept. In Greek tradition, the Great God Pan was Lord and ruler of wild solitary places. If intruded upon (particularly if taking a nap) he would release

a cry, inducing sheer terror. His name was given to the word to describe the dread: panic.

The disorientation of being lost within a familiar landscape might entice us to feel this primordial anxiety. Perhaps this is an ancient experience of being human with the land.

Breaking the Spell

Earliest sources suggest carrying a cross or a piece of bread will end the enchantment. Sir John and Lady Fitz broke the spell by drinking from a spring in 1568. But hands down the most popular remedy to break the Pixie spell is to invert an item of clothing.

Why turn clothing? Bray suggests it is because the Pixies 'can't stand the sight of anyone improperly dressed' (Bray, 1836). An early reference to someone being Pixy-led (*c*.1750) proposed, 'it gives a person time to recollect himself' (Halliwell, 1846).

PIXIE LIGHTS

Exmoor, Somerset

Turn your cloaks, for Fairy folks are in old Oaks!

Old saying, England

There used to be a meadow in Porlock Vale on Exmoor where little lights could be seen burning at night. 'Don't look at them,' people said, but one night an unlucky woman stopped and looked at those fires. She saw shadows moving around them and realised they were Pixies. They looked like root silhouettes.

She saw Pixies dressing their children in the lights of the fire. The Pixies caught her looking and were terribly angry. They shot towards her so fast she did not have time to turn her cloak. They led her on a wild chase through the marshy bog, into the woods, over the hills and down vales, and they did not release her 'til daybreak.

VOYAGE WITH THE PISKIES

Polperro, Cornwall

Careful how you go, you just don't know who is nearby in these ancient hedges. Sometimes, however, what awaits is not all that bad after all …

Another version of this story, 'The Piskies in the Cellar', is told in Cornwall by Hunt. He used Quiller-Couch as his source and likened the story to 'The Cluricaun' and 'The Haunted Cellar' in Fairy Legends and Traditions of the South of Ireland *by T. Crofton Crocker.*

I have worked from Quiller-Couch's father's version, although the story Hunt recorded does have a ridiculously pleasing ending in which, instead of coming home, the voyager gets caught in the cellar and sentenced to death. Facing the gallows, he hears a little voice, saying 'I'm for …'

Polperro is nestled in Talland Bay and about half a mile east is the little hamlet of Portallow. A scattering of houses surround a green where for hundreds of years children have met and played.

The village boy, who was newly employed on a farm, looked out towards the green and saw his friends playing. Last week he would have joined them, but the farmer's wife had sent him on errands all the way to Polperro so there was no time to play.

The dimpsy time had crept up while he had delivered his mistress's letter and bundled the supplies into a package. He hadn't even begun to scale the big hill back up to Portallow when the last light of twilight ebbed away.

He had reached Sand-hill when he heard a voice in the dark, 'I'm for Portallow Green.'

Some company would be very welcome he thought – it surely would make the dark lanes less frightful.

'I'm for Portallow Green,' the boy replied quickly, intending to let his fellow traveller know he was there.

Quicker than a thought, he found himself on Portallow Green. Surrounded by a throng of laughing Piskies!

He burst out laughing and the merriment rippled across the green. If only the other children were here to see this.

After a moment a few voices chimed together, 'I'm for Seaton Beach.'

'I'm for Seaton Beach,' he echoed. Faster than a flash, he appeared with the merry crowd of Piskies on that beautiful stretch of beach towards Rame Head.

He had always been told the Piskies were dangerous, but they were such merry spirits, dancing and making music with gay abandon in circles. Besides, surely this was the finest way to travel. The boy put down the package under his arm, threw his hands into the air and joined in the revel, dancing circles into the whistling wind.

'I'm for the King of France's cellar,' said a Piskey voice – and without letting a moment slide he called out, 'I'm for the King of France's cellar.' Sure enough, before his heart could beat again, the merry travelling party found themselves in the most decadent cellar one could imagine.

Barrels and casks of wine and liquor were stacked higher than he could see and soon the best of it was flowing, and the merry crowd tasted the richest treasures of France.

The merriment continued with dancing and music and all the while they laughed.

The revelling throng led the lad up into the palace. They went through state rooms and through apartments of such opulence he could barely believe it. As he was passing a table laid with the finest porcelain, crystal glass, silver and gold, he held a small cup and wondered at it.

A voice called the voyage on: 'I'm for Seaton Beach.' The boy looked up and chimed his reply. In a blink of an eye, there they all were again, back under the stars, dancing on the beach.

The lad still had the cup in his hand. He slid it into his pocket and remembered his own package that he had left on the beach. It was exactly where he had left it all that while before.

'I'm for Portallow Green,' came the chorus and he responded, finding himself back on his home turf again. The lad took a step out of the circle and let the journeying Piskies travel on, dancing their circles off into the night.

Relieved to be home with the package under his arm, he walked into the farmhouse and was greeted with a warm embrace. 'Well done my boy,' said the mistress. 'You made excellent time!'

'But, I've been hours! If you only knew where I've been and what I've seen! I've been all the way to France. To the King's own cellar.' And with great excitement he told his story.

'Well, it seems we have a right and proper storyteller. Have you been drinking, my boy?' the mistress looked at him disapprovingly.

The boy pulled the silver cup out of his back pocket.

'I'm not making it up. Look!'

The farmer and his wife examined it, and after much wonder and incredulity they believed the boy's story.

The cup stayed at the farm and remained the property of the lad's family for generations.

THE TALE OF JOAN THE WAD AND JACK O'LANTERN

by Holly Ebony (2018)

As I was out a-walking on the dark and gloomy moor
so miserable and misty, I could barely see the path before me,
Suddenly ahead I saw, a warm and welcome sight,
the flickering and glowing of a most inviting light.
But as I tried to seek its source, it seemed to dance away,
leaping one way then the other. I was led astray,
wading right up to my middle in gorse and tangle, bog and trouble
my path long gone, my boots a puddle. Then the light snuffed out!

Then out there leapt a laughing woman, tiny as a child.
She patted me upon my knee, and giggling she cried;

'Jack, oh Jack, oh Jack O'Lantern! Will-o'-the, Will-o'-the-Wisp.
We've had our fun, but our game is done, my husband dear desist.
Joan, oh Joan, oh Joan the Wad! The Pixie Queen am I,
I love to play, but you've lost your way, fear not, I shall assist,
follow, follow, follow, follow, follow my guiding light,
sing along, and I'll lead you home on this dark and stormy night.

'Jack, oh Jack, oh Jack O'Lantern! Will-o'-the, Will-o'-the-Wisp.
We've had our fun, but our game is done. My husband dear desist.
Joan, oh Joan, oh Joan the Wad! The Pixie Queen am I!
I love to play, but you've lost your way, fear not, I shall assist,
follow, follow, follow, follow, follow my guiding light,
sing along, and I'll lead you home on this dark and stormy night.
On this dark and stormy night!'

JAN COO

Dartmoor, Devon

High up on the moor, the twin streams of East and West Dart converge in a grand dance at Dartmeet and flow as one great body through the most stunning valley south towards Newbridge. The ancient river's voice pummels through the rocky valley and has become famous as a grade 5 white water route among adventure-seeking kayakers.

Oak and birch grow majestically above the river and cloak the air below, their branches green with moss and rare lichens. Walking anywhere along this stretch of river is a delight. But be careful if you want to cross the river, it is hungrier than you think.

There is a farmhouse called Rowbrook, positioned below the distinctive point of Sharp Tor and standing above Luckey Tor in the Dart Valley.

At this farm a lad was once employed to care for the cattle. He was a quiet boy and had been through a lot, but after working nearly twelve months he had proved himself as an efficient worker and a friendly companion.

One evening, in the winter season, he came hurrying into the warm farmhouse obviously upset.

'There's someone in the valley calling in distress,' he exclaimed.

The farm labourers jumped up from beside the peat fire and agreed someone must have lost their way: 'per'aps some fool tried crossing the river?'

They jumped into action and went down through the fields to where the lad had heard the call.

In winter the Dart valley is painted brown and purple by the leafless oak and birch trees. All the spectators looked through the naked branches for any sign of a lost soul.

Nothing but the sound of the river could be heard and after a while the party decided the lad must be mistaken. Just as they turned to go, they heard an urgent voice call, 'Jan Coo! Jan Coo.'

The voice was no distance at all. They all set out in search, along the pathways they knew, down to the river. They searched and called out to the voice, but it did not reply. As the light began to fade, the group of them drew back together and agreed it was strange indeed.

The next night the lad ran into the kitchen just the same, and excitedly he told them he had heard the voice again. They leapt up and went to where the boy had heard the voice. They had hardly been there a minute when they heard, 'Jan Coo! Jan Coo!'

'Where are you?'

'Are you lost?'

'Do you need help?'

There was no reply to any of them, but the voice continued to call out again and again, 'Jan Coo! Jan Coo!'

When they all got back around the fire that night the eldest among them mumbled, 'Tis the Pisgies, I'll warn. They say you can't hear the difference between one of them and a Christian. We best leave alone.'

'Es, that's what it is for sure. We had better leave 'em be.'

'I don't want none of you lot being Pixy-led,' said the mistress of the house.

'That's that then,' they agreed. 'If we hear it again, we leave 'em be.'

But the voice was heard again and again.

The lad couldn't help but listen out for it. He felt like it was calling to him. It was unsettling, and yet somehow powerfully alluring.

Winter was nearly through and the primroses were shining their strange light upon the pathways across the moor. The lad and the farmer's son were out in the fields when the voice called out again, 'Jan Coo!'

The lad replied, 'Jan Coo!' and quickly the voice called again, 'Jan Coo! Jan Coo!'

'Leave it,' said the farmer's son, 'You know it's not human.'

'It's coming from Langamarsh Pit on the other side of the river. I'll just take a little look.'

Before his companion could dissuade him, the lad had gone, jumping from rock to rock, down the steepest part of the valley towards the river.

The farmer's son returned to the house, hearing the voice call out continually, 'Jan Coo, Jan Coo, Jan Coo, Jan Coo!' Until he put his hand on the latch and the voice fell silent.

The boy turned suddenly, but it did not call out again.

He went inside and told them all about the voice and that the lad had gone looking for it.

Hour after hour passed and the lad did not come back. When it started to get dark they all went out, calling his name, but there was silence in the valley. No lad, no strange voice.

He was never seen again.

'The Pisgies got their prize tonight,' an old man muttered.

'That, or the river took its yearly charge,' said another.

River Dart, oh River Dart!
Every year you claim a heart.

TARR BALL AND THE FARMER

Exmoor, Somerset

We've not even mentioned Robin Goodfellow yet! How rude!

He was Britain's most notorious mischief-making Fairy, influencing Shakespeare, Dickens and Kipling. In a document published in 1628 we are shown Robin's folklore and the stories are strikingly similar to Pixie tales. It is very probable that, regardless of whether your local mischievous spirits were Pixies, Boggarts or Brownies, your tricksters were likely taught by the best.

Robin Goodfellow's idea of merry jests included: leading people astray and laughing at them, cleaning the home/expecting a freshly swept hearth, and helping thresh corn. Remind you of anyone? Robin was able to transform himself into whatever image suited him best.

In this story we see a Fairy take the shape of (multiple) bulls. Farmers, take note! Again we see a Pixie interfering with the livestock. Cattle seem to be their favourites!

Let's be honest. He was a tight old bastard.

'Old Curmudgeon' his servants called him. Very first night he moved into that big old farm at Lucott he questioned why the servants put out water and a dish of his finest cream.

'Tradition. Tis for the Pisgies! We are on the edge of Hawkcombe woods after all.'

'Not in my house.' And that was that.

No matter how hard the servants worked the next day, in house and stables, their work was never done. Triple they all worked, and still there was more to do the next day. Each of them knew why of course. But Old Curmudgeon didn't see the warning. No water, no cream again, nor the next night.

So, they came for him.

Next evening he went out to the top lawn to bring in the four young heifers he had spent a pretty penny on. They were wild, and even to the crack of his own whip they disobeyed. Off they galloped down the rocky lane, past Lucott hill, over Nutscale Ford and up on to Tarr Ball.

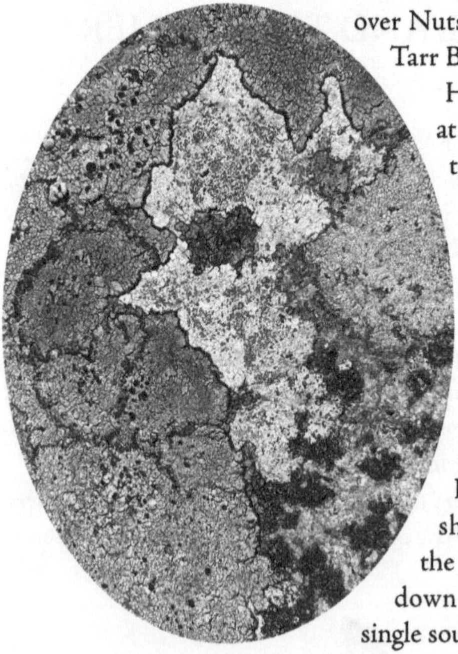

He shouted blue murder at those cows, loud enough to wake up the farmers over the far side of Exmoor, but no one heard him. Shouting himself hoarse, not a single soul heard his cries, as if some sort of barrier blocked him off from his neighbours. Even as he went past the shepherd's cottage, past the mill and all the cottages down at Little Combe, not a single soul heard him.

Up and down Nutscale Ford he went, back and forth chasing those damn heifers. The Pixies laughed from every hole, every crack in the ground in that uncanny cleeve.

At points he forgot what he was chasing, but he continued ever on, speeding past hedge and briar, down pathways he would never see again. Until he came out at Tarr Ball and spotted his heifers. He gave chase but a mist rolled in and they disappeared again.

Laughter seemed to surround him, but as soon as he slowed his horse he couldn't tell from where it was coming.

And so it went on, all night. Some say the Pixies took him out of time that night and punished him a lifetime in a night for his neglect. Whatever it was, when the sun came up and he made his way through the gorse patch path down Babe Hill, he was older and withered, bruised and torn, soaked to the bare skin. When he approached the house, his servants called out to their master, asking what troubled him?

'The heifers,' he managed to say. But the stable hand came out to say the four fine heifers were fed and happy in the stable, where they had been all night.

PIXY AT THE OCKERY

Dartmoor, Devon

When dusk falls across the South West it's called 'dimpsy' time. Growing up on the edge of the moor, it was instilled in me to be home well before darkness falls.

This is perfectly sensible of course: trip over a stone, a root or a hole and you can easily twist an ankle. If you have no mobile signal on the moor you might get stuck just before the temperature plummets.

But the real reason is even more dangerous … the dimpsy is when the spirits come out and their time begins. Best to be off their path unless something unwanted is invited to happen.

The sun set over the western side of the moor and as the golden sky turned pink, the light began to dim fast. 'Dangerously fast', thought a woman making her way home to Princetown after a long journey. She held her basket close to her body as she crossed the West Dart at Two Bridges. She was only a mile and a half away, but she knew the light would not last the journey.

She walked faster and faster through the dimpsy light, but she knew it wasn't safe to walk too quickly through the darkness. A wrong step could twist an ankle or a short cut could lead you into boggy ground in a moment. But it wasn't a twisted ankle she was worried about; she could hear her grandma's voice in her head, 'Be home before the dimpsy time, for then the Piskies are at play.'

She continued walking as carefully as she could. 'I know the road,' she told herself, 'and I will be home in half an hour.' But this was Piskey time, and she knew it.

Something darted on to the path up in front of her. Was it a fox, or a dog? It moved far too fast to be a sheep, and it seemed to leap and gambol in its step.

It laughed as it leapt and she knew then it was a Pixy.

She hesitated, not knowing what to do. She couldn't turn round, not now that she was so close to home. To avoid misfortune, she inverted her shawl as she had no pockets to turn inside out.

Plucking up her courage, she continued walking, holding tightly to her basket, and continued onwards as the light dimmed more and more.

Through the thickening darkness she could see without doubt, the Pixy about 8 inches tall. It had stopped on the Ockery bridge that crossed the Blackabrook on its way to the West Dart. Mist was rolling in from the mires, cloaking the furthest side of the bridge. She was so very close to home now.

The Pixie leapt nimbly from one side of the bridge to the other, backwards and forwards, faster and faster. She had the idea it was taunting her. The Pixie moved so fast it created a shaded arch, like a darkened rainbow across the water.

Surely it was a trap. She did not want to be Pixy-led, but she was only ten minutes away from Princeton now.

Refusing to turn around, she felt her courage and leant into it.

She walked towards her fear and felt something plucky in her that reminded her of her own dear grandma.

As she stepped on to the bridge, the Pixy landed right beside her, and without any forethought she grabbed the creature, opened her basket and bundled it into the cramped space, closing the lid and fastening it shut.

She sped so quickly up that road.

The most extraordinary voice cried out in protest and alarm. She could not understand a word it spoke, but it was clearly furious.

'It's no good you going on like that,' she said, 'I won't be Pixy-led tonight. Have you ever been Human-led? I dare say this might be a first,' she chuckled to herself. 'You'd best get comfy in there.'

As she walked, the tone of voice inside the basket changed to something slightly more … merry? A stream of chattering, giggling words flowed from her basket as quickly as moving water.

'You sound like the river at full flood. The children at home will be delighted to see you.'

As she stepped under the lights of Princetown and approached home, the basket drew more and more quiet until no sound could be heard at all. Suddenly a fear came upon the woman: what if it was still furious? What if it might pull a prank on her own dear children? Or, God forbid, what if it had died in her basket?

Under a street lamp she undid the basket's buckle and opened the lid an inch, but there was no Pixy inside.

When she finally reached home she told her children and husband about her incredible encounter. 'I just don't know how it could have got out,' she said to them all.

'Maybe it turned into a fly?' said one of her daughters 'Maybe a flea?' said another. They looked around the room, just in case.

'Perhaps it is safest for both Piskie and human that it did not find its way into our home tonight!' her husband said, laughing, 'But the courage to catch a Piskie? There's not many who can claim that!'

4

ALLURING LIGHTS: MIDNIGHT MISCHIEF

The day has faded into night, the stars are shining and the Pixies are out.

Do you dare go outside? Do you dare speak their name?

The superstition that Fairies (or supernatural beings) gained power over someone by using their name is present in Celtic and European mythology. It was believed that names were linked to the vital essence of a person's soul.

The idea can be traced back to ancient Egypt, where pharaohs often had secret names. The idea is seen again in Jewish tradition in the legend of the Gollum of Prague. In the story, Rabbi Loew brought a clay humanoid figure to life using secret knowledge of God's true name.

The superstition persisted in medieval Christianity, blending ideas and fears of demons and angels.

It is a device continued in modern fantasy (Le Guin's *A Wizard of Earthsea* is a fine example), where knowing someone or something's true name gives the possessor power over it. To speak a word is to call it into your attention, and to call its attention to you. Words are a magical thing.

It's likely this is why we have so many names to affectionately describe our magical neighbours, who may manipulate us at their whim or fancy. I have met people today who are careful to speak the name 'Pixie' aloud. They will tell you it is safest to call them the Little People, the People of the Hills, the Shining Ones, or the Good Neighbours.

Watch out! If you're in Pixie territory, expect mischief!

ON THE MARE'S NECK

Bodmin Moor, Cornwall

There are very few Piskey stories that I have found from Bodmin Moor, although the Piskey vibes there are strong. Sabine Baring-Gould got himself stuck in a mire at the base of Rough Tor and luckily one of his party went the wrong way and found him, otherwise the song-collecting reverend may have had a tricksy sticky Piskey ending.

In the writing of Nellie Sloggett (publishing under Enys Tregarthen) we have this story from Bodmin that seems like it might be inspired by an oral folk tale. It was included in Pixie Folklore and Legends, *published after Sloggett's death by Elizabeth Yates, who references Sloggett's note that it was a 'family story'.*

It was well known and well documented that Pixies were prone to stealing a horse, pony or a colt and riding it half to death. It would be interesting to map the reports of exhausted horses to see if they were found along known smuggling routes.

Josey Tregaskis was a farmer who lived on a farm in 'the granite district' on the northern side of Bodmin. He had taken his horse, Bess, to Camelford for market day, and it was a good day to be in town, so he stayed a while.

It was late when he got back to Bess and he apologised for keeping her waiting. He didn't need to; she was happy riding at day or night.

It was nearly midnight as they made their way out on to the open moor. Bess was visibly glad to be out of the narrow lanes and she sped up in pleasure. She liked the wind in her hair – the moor was her home.

As they dipped down into a hill, Bess whinnied and her ears pricked up. 'What's the matter, old girl?' Josey said, slowing her down, then he saw them. Little lights darted across the moor, 'The Piskeys are out tonight. Riding their colts.'

He had seen the lights before so he wasn't too surprised, but he brought her up to a canter all the same. 'Let's get home!'

They rode on and when they passed the furze break, Josey saw the strangest thing. Three little lights leapt right up on to Bess's head. Lights the size of lark's eggs shone on to the little Piskeys holding them, two between her ears, the other on the crest of her neck. They were whiskered little men, wearing red hats and green jackets, and were about the size of a thumb.

Josey was amazed, but they didn't take a bit of notice of him. Their hands were creased and aged and they had mischief in their eyes. He suddenly wondered if something terrible was about to happen. He knew Piskeys liked to run a pony ragged. For a moment he thought about flicking them off, but he was miles from home still; it was too unsafe.

Josey slowed Bess down to a steady trot, and Bess made some funny noises, like she did with her colts. She was having words with the Piskeys. The Piskeys started talking to each other and though he couldn't understand what they said, he could hear their laughter clear enough.

What should he do? He became more and more anxious something awful might happen. At that point, one of the Piskeys tickled

Bess's ear. Was the little man trying to get Bess to kick him off? As he thought it, the Piskey turned and gave him a rueful glare that looked like it meant, 'Wouldn't it be funny if we did?'

Bess cantered on as steady as ever. After a few more miles, they got close enough to home and his dog heard them and barked in pleasure. The Piskeys disappeared then, their lights out, though he could still hear them talking. Bess brought them into the farm and up to the gate, when Josey heard the laughing get quieter and quieter behind him. The little people had left them. They had made it home!

'Well I never did,' he laughed as he hugged Bess as tight as he ever had. He took off the saddle and gave her a great scratching in gratitude. As he was brushing her, he saw that her mane was plaited into little tails, with looped stirrups and even little panniers woven into her hair.

'I knew they were up to something. I think we got home just in time.'

He gave her extra hay that night and Bess replied with a very pleased whinny that seemed to say, 'Did you ever doubt me?'

TULIP PIXIES

Tavistock, Devon

The following tale was recorded in 1832 by Anna Eliza Bray in her letters to Poet Laureate Robert Southey. The letters were published in 1836 in three volumes. It is within these pages that the stories of the Pixies made their way out of the South West and caught the imagination of a far wider audience. As Victoria took to the throne in 1838, heralding a new era, the Pixies ran through the imaginations of Britain and its empire.

Among these stories there is a repeated pattern of older female characters and the Pixies. I had the privilege of growing up with an enchanting grannie who had a very similar garden to the one in this story. It makes a lot of sense to me that a special kind of magic is gifted to us by our grandparents.

This story was first told to me by the wonderful Dartmoor-based storyteller Sara Hurley. I now pass it on to you.

On the outskirts of Tavistock, there was a Pixie field.

For countless years it continued to be a favourite haunt of the Pixies, where they would meet in the dead of night and hold their revels.

In the morning, circles of lush grass could be spied by sharp eyes, revealing where the spirits had danced the night before.

Next to this special spot lived an old woman in a little cottage. She loved it there as much as the Pixies did. She had seen the circles many times and knew what they meant.

She poured her love into the garden and often talked to the plants and all the life she encountered there. Those plants grew wild, lush and abundant, filling the garden with depth and colour at all times of the year.

There grew lavender and hollyhocks, lilies and rosemary, primrose, blue buttons, gillyflowers, forget-me-nots and rue.

In the flower bed below the window of her little cottage she tended the most extraordinary bed of tulips.

Travellers to Tavistock market would stop when they reached her cottage and look over the wall, and if she was there they would always comment on those tulips.

'How do you do it? Never before have I seen such big flowers. If that was a glass of red wine, I'd be drunk!'

One evening, in the dead of night, she lay in bed not able to sleep, though she felt like she must be dreaming. The most curious sound out of the window kept her awake. It was as if the voices of the birds and the rivers were singing in golden duet, carried on a breeze. It was a sweet, haunting lullaby.

She thought she must have dreamt it, but the next night it came again.

On the third night, she did not go to bed. She left the downstairs window open, just a slight, and waited to see if she could identify where the song was coming from …

She watched as the stars came out and the moon rose. The garden was filled with darkness and light. The old woman nearly gasped as she watched small, shadowy figures holding bundles dart across the garden towards her.

They approached the tulip bed that grew beneath the window she hid behind.

Amazed, it dawned on her that they were Pixies. Real-life Pixies! She watched as they uncovered the bundles, revealing tiny elfin babies.

They cradled their babes in the bowl of each tulip, and sang into the petals.

On their breath was a song of enchantment, as beautiful as it was beguiling. When the parent had finished its extraordinary song, the song looped, lingering in the flower, while the tulip gently rocked its special parcel without the need for a breeze.

Another Pixie did the same and then another, until every single tulip contained an elfin baby. When everyone was lulled to sleep, the Pixies ran out across the garden, over the wall and into the neighbouring field that was their moon meadow. The old lady watched them dancing in their circles.

'Well, bless me!' the old woman said, going back to bed, not wanting to intrude on the magic folk. She couldn't sleep for the excitement.

Before the first light of dawn, the Pixies returned to collect their babies, and she could hear them kissing and caressing their children even after they turned invisible in the rising light.

The tulips themselves were proud to be trusted with this special charge. The breath of the Pixies enabled the plants to grow taller and to keep their beauty for longer. They even became as fragrant as roses.

So delighted was the old woman that the Pixies should bless her garden in this way, she gave special attention to the tulip bed. Not a single tulip was ever plucked from its stem, and they were always given the best compost.

The moon cycled continually, and while the Pixies could always be trusted to return, the time came when the old woman smelled the tulips for the last time.

After her funeral, the house was sold and the new owner did not think to smell the tulips. He had plans for the garden and immediately pulled out the plants they did not want.

Out went the tulip bulbs, in went a bed of parsley.

The garden, which had been rich with root and bloom, became a barren lawn.

When the spring came, the Pixies returned to the garden with their baby bundles and were horrified to see the destruction these people had made to their sacred space.

They were so grieved and offended, they sank into the roots and sang a song of undoing. All the parsley withered away. Indeed, for many years not a single thing grew in any part of that garden.

But the Pixies did not forget the kindness the old woman had shown them.

In the dead of night, the Pixies were heard lamenting and singing dirges around the grave that wrapped her body.

There they would pay tribute to her memory before the moon was full.

No human hand ever tended to the old woman's grave but no plant grew there out of place. The grass was as green as a Pixie ring, and the prettiest flowers sprung up without sewing or planting. There was rosemary and gillyflowers, lavender and forget-me-nots, sweet scabious and rue, all blooming between the most stunning tulips that Tavistock has ever known.

NO SUPPER, NO GOLD!

Dartmoor, Devon

This story comes from the south-western rural reaches of inner Dartmoor, near the Plym Head. Here ancient settlements and modern tin workings reveal the traces of our ancestors. Near the old mine at Eylesbarrow it is possible to discover some old chambers, still visible today, where potatoes were stored to keep them fresh. William Crossing suggests that a bottle or two of smuggled spirits may well have found their way into these storage places …

Only a gentle breeze teased Dartmoor that night. The silver moon shone, scattering the moor with dancing shadows between granite and bracken. The labourer walked along the tin workings, down the side of Eylesbarrow, not far from Combeshead Farm.

I cannot say why the man was walking there that night, all I know is that he jumped out of his skin when he heard the sounds of voices near him. He froze as if caught red-handed.

Moving cautiously forward, he peeped over the side of a gully and peered down to see who was there.

It took a moment for his eyes to settle, but small movements gave them away … an endless group of Pixies were down there, hard at work among the tin spoils. He watched a whole host of them stream along with picks and axes, pointing and discussing, going this way and that. Some pushed wheelbarrows full with gravel, others were lifting, moving rocks, or sweeping paths.

The man watched a Pixie climb up the edge of the gully just a foot away from his left ear and call out to the Pixies below, 'Time for supper!'

Every Pixy in the gully downed tools and turned towards the caller.

Heart beating fast, the man held his nerve and spoke as nonchalantly as he could.

'Ess, I should say twas time vur supper. If you'm zo hungered as I. But, uhhhrm, what be diggin' vur?'

'Tin,' replied the Pixie.

'Helpin' our the miners be 'e? Why daun't 'e dig vur goold? I'd vill my pockets vull.'

'After supper!' said the Pixy. 'No supper, no gold.'

'Then I'll ave zum zupper wi' 'e and pick the gold arterwards.'

The ground gave way beneath him and, impelled by a force far beyond gravity, he was dropped into the earth through the hill. Streams of Pixies swarmed around him until his feet gently met the ground, and he found himself in the most amazing subterranean cavern.

'T'was a gert hall like wan o' they up nigh Combeshaid Tar,' as he described it afterwards.

Here the Pixies were preparing a feast. Minikin liquids balanced on leaves and bitty berries were brought in on platters no bigger than a penny. Miniature glazed grasshopper hams and swirls of honey on thorns made the most spectacular display. A feast of tiny proportions, laid out in front of them all.

The labourer wondered if there was anything slightly more … substantial coming, some bacon, perhaps? He knew the Pixies loved a pasty.

A large steaming kettle hung over the fire on a three-legged brandis. The sweetest smell of stew issued forth, exciting a crowd of Pixies around it.

The man got up to take a closer look.

'Take care! Take care!' cried a Pixy as his footsteps towered over the little ones. 'Don't knock over the …'

But the legs of the triangular utensil were not where he thought they had been and the legs gave way, emptying the kettle on to the fire, which roared and hissed as it died, billowing stew-soaked smoke.

'No supper, no gold,' chorused the spirits as everything went dark. His body propelled upwards faster than the wind, until he hit the ground face first with a thud. When he came to his senses, he was in the gully, where he had first spied the little spirits.

'Drat those little toads wi' their no zupper, no goold. There bant n'ither vur me, that's a zartin thing.'

FISHERMAN AND THE PISKEYS

Polperro, Cornwall

Polperro is an ancient fishing village on the south coast of Cornwall. The narrow streets wind down to the harbour where the picturesque village meets the tidal sea, held back by the breakwater. It has a rich history of fishing, smuggling and Piskeys.

Home to Joan the Wad, Queen of the Cornish Piskies, the village still has a wonderful Joan the Wad Piskey Headquarters shop, where you can get lucky charms and a great welcome from Mike and Jenny.

The Piskeys delight in their mischief and value their solitude, but in Polperro the Piskeys have developed a much closer relationship with their human neighbours. It is said they bring endless luck, but this also means nonstop tricks on generations of residents.

A fisherman told this to Jonathan Couch. I have slightly modified the ending, based on Couch's notes.

Once upon a time there was a fisherman named John Taprail who lived in a little cottage in Polperro. He had heard that the winds might be high that night, so he moored his boat next to a barge of a much larger size, which would keep it shielded very nicely.

Home and pleased with himself, he slept soundly until a voice woke him, urging him up out of bed. 'Get up! Get up! Shift the ropes. Tangle, tear and crush! The boat is in danger!'

In an instant, he was in his boots, wrapped in his coat, hat on hurtling down the street towards the harbour. He was down by the water before he realised the wind wasn't blowing. Much to his annoyance, he realised he'd been tricked; both his boat and the barge next to it were safe, softly riding their ropes.

Turning for home, he heard voices coming from an upturned boat, on the edge of the beach.

He lowered his head to see who was about, and was surprised to see a group of small folk sitting in a semicircle. Each one of them held out their hats, while one of them distributed a heap of gold coins between them.

John threw his hat into the circle before he had time to stop himself. Amazingly it landed without rousing suspicion. Delighted, he saw some glinting gold coins land in his hat as the wealth was shared equally. John held his nerve as long as he dared, but he knew he would be punished if discovered. Very carefully he withdrew his hat, slipped the coins in his pocket and made off for home. He had got a head start before he was discovered, but the Piskies flooded out from under the boat, hot on his heels.

John ran home as fast as he could, and when slamming the door behind him, he trapped his coat tails in the door.

The angry crowd outside wrenched and pulled at the tails of the trapped fabric.

Caught in the door, he knew the best way to get rid of the intruders was to invert his pocket. As he did, the coins fell out and vanished, along with the Piskeys.

5

CIRCLE MAGIC: GALLITRAPS AND PIXY RINGS

They're colourful, enchanting and beguiling … and, some of them can kill you. Not the Pixies … for a moment, let's delve into the world of fungi.

Mushrooms and toadstools are the fruiting bodies of grand networks of mycelium that exist in sophisticated networks beneath the earth's surface.

Some fungi grow in circles and can be spotted as areas of darker green grass under certain trees or in grassy fields. As the subterranean mycelium grows, it expands outwards, releasing chemicals that break down organic matter, fertilising the ground where it lives with nutrient riches. This is advantageous to the grass, which is why it grows greener where the fungi reside.

In folklore these circles are entrances to the other world. In the South West they are known as Pixy rings, gallitraps or Fairy rings.

Some believed that the dark green circles were made by the Pixies riding young colts in circles during the night. Others believed that the circles reveal the locations where the Little Folk had been dancing. Other writers have suggested that Pixy rings reveal 'entrances to hoards of subterranean treasures' (King, 1856, p.75). In Somerset it was understood that if anyone stepped into a gallitrap with one foot, they would see the Fairies but could escape. If that person was unfortunate enough to put both feet inside the ring, they would be totally in the power of the Pixies (Tongue, 1965, p.114). However, if a thief or murderer sets foot in the ring, he will end on the gallows (Briggs and Tongue, 1965, p.51).

Old folklore attests that running around a Fairy ring nine times on the first night of the full moon reveals the sounds of hilarity and celebration from the underground abode of the elves (Wright, 1914, p.208). One day the Rev Hawker of Morwenstow warned a lady from Bude not to pick a mushroom in a circle. She neglected his warning and within a week her daughter died (Baring-Gould, *The Vicar of Morwenstow*, 1876, p.164).

The image of a Pixie is synonymous with a toadstool. Depictions of a Pixie seated on a toadstool holding their knees is a repeated image found on endless charms, souvenirs and Pixie memorabilia. Most often, they are depicted sitting on the red and white fly agaric mushroom. This image is an instant visual signifier of magic and the Fairy realms, and was depicted prolifically by Victorian Fairy artists. The influence continues today.

Let's not ignore the effect of psychedelic mushrooms, which will relax the doors of your perception and enter you into an 'otherworld'. The fly agaric contains psychoactive properties, as do liberty caps, commonly found across the South West and often featuring in depictions of Pixies.

If you don't know whether the fungus in your hand is dinner, a death sentence, or a magical peep into the otherworld, you'd better get some advice from someone who does.

Be careful. Learn your field mushroom from your destroying angel.

HUCCABY COURTING

Dartmoor, Devon

Some say the path to true love is a rocky road … The chances of you spiralling out of control until the very essence of you is undone is highly unlikely, but it's never impossible.

You never know what you might find on Dartmoor.

Deep into Dartmoor, on the eastern side of the West Dart River, just above Hexworthy bridge is Huccaby Farm. Many, many years ago, there was a fine young woman called Mary who worked in the dairy there. She was as beautiful as she was clever. Mary caused such a stir one spring when she was heard saying she wanted to find a beau. It seemed that every single person from Mary Tavy to Moretonhampstead presented themselves as a suitor. She had a record number of cards and flowers and proposals from suitors attempting to capture her attention.

It was Tom White who impressed her beyond all others, and after she made it known, the other suitors left the two lovers to a summer of courting.

Tom worked on a farm in Postbridge and never had much time off, but after his work was done and his dinner eaten, he would make the 5-mile journey to see his sweetheart.

The 5 miles to Huccaby went by very quickly, with thoughts of Mary on his mind. The journey home always felt much further as he mentally prepared for work the coming day. Regardless, the journey was always worth it. Mary was clever and witty and so very kind. Tom felt he was the luckiest person on the moor.

He liked the way she left fresh flowers for her masters on their dining table and the kind way she referred to the cows that she milked.

Mary liked that Tom was such a hard worker and so dedicated to visiting her, even though it was a 10-mile round trip for him, which he made multiple times a week.

Tom knew he wanted to marry her, and he worked up his confidence over that summer to ask her.

One summer evening he had journeyed from Postbridge to see his Mary, and had stayed out extra late with her.

He had wanted to pop the question, but in waiting for the right moment, he had delayed and delayed and finally he bottled out and bid her goodnight. He walked away that night sorely disappointed.

He climbed up the hill, annoyed with himself, and doubly frustrated. The sky was lightening and dawn would arrive far sooner than he wished. He realised he wasn't going to get much sleep that night.

Walking faster now, he tried to get back to Postbridge with at least a little time to close his eyes before another day of labour began. He walked so fast he didn't hear the noise as early as he might. But finally the sound of music and laughter met his ears.

'How queer,' he thought as the wind blew it away, 'who on earth could be keeping revels at such an hour?' He decided it must surely be a trick of the wind.

The looming shapes of Believer Tor appeared out of the blanket of night, casting strange and fantastical forms and causing him to stand still in wonder.

As he strained to see the shapes, the laughing returned, louder than ever and so very near.

Curiously, he walked towards the rocks and made his way around to the little green grassy patch below the towering tor.

Too late, he walked out and saw a whole host of the most fabulously dressed little elven Pixies holding a grand revel on the grassy spot. They seemed to make their own light, which emanated from the circle where they danced. The illumination shone upon Pixies sitting all over the great granite tor, playing instruments and laughing.

Tom froze, 'Pixies!' he said under his breath. He tried to retreat without being seen, but tripped on a stone, revealing his presence.

In a flash the circle appeared around him and the elven spirits danced around him faster and faster, laughing all the while.

He tried to resist the dance; he had heard tales of people who had been caught in the ring of a Pixie circle who had not been able to escape for a year and a day, but he could not resist! The music was so enticing and the speed of the dance grew faster and faster; it spun him around on the spot.

'Stop it! Please!' he cried, but their laughter grew and they sped faster until they were at such a pace that everything became a blur. Tom spun faster than a spinning top. The landscape melted into lines of colours, ideas unravelled, atoms seemed to separate from their forms. Every part of Tom was being undone. Yet still their laughter grew and grew until it felt as if all of space were laughing at him, eardrums about to explode.

In the height of the wild moment, the first light of golden sun appeared from the ridge of Hamel Down and as the first ray of light spilt over to Bellever Tor, the Pixies vanished and their laughter ceased.

Tom was released from the dance and fell to the ground completely exhausted.

He was shaken by the experience, and although he had never missed a day of work, it took him a long time to crawl back home. He was bedridden for days, and when he was strong enough to return to work, he promised he would never go courting again for fear of what he might find crossing the moors in the dark.

Poor Mary waited in vain for her lover to return.

Tom was true to his word and remained a bachelor for the rest of his life. Mary, on the other hand, did not have any trouble attracting more suitors.

A saying often heard on Dartmoor is, 'When gorse is out of bloom, kissing is out of fashion'. Lucky for us all, gorse is always in flower somewhere.

AT THE END OF TRESIDDER LANE

West Penwith, Cornwall

Their merry wakes and pastimes keep:
What hath night to do with sleep?

John Milton

As the sun sank beneath the rooftops of Penzance, Mr Trezillian began his journey home. It was an hour to ride the 10 miles home and he would be in the dark for the most of it. Still, his horse was well rested and he knew the way.

His ride took him west to Tresidder, through a stretch of West Penwith that was well populated with 'Small Folk', as his neighbours called them. He knew the stories, and was sure there was nothing more to them than fanciful romance.

After all, these gullible people said that the spirits liked to hold their fairs on his very doorstep, at the end of Tresidder Lane. He had never seen anything. Well, nothing apart from those dark circles in the grass.

At last, he came near the entrance to Tresidder Lane, but as he did he caught sight of swift movements on the green. He paused, wanting to know what his tired eyes were seeing. Sure enough, there were little bodies, figures the size of rabbits, holding hands, dancing. Round and round.

What a queer thing, The longer he watched, the more able he was to see their merriment. An incredible desire to join them came over him, and without realising what he was doing, he slid off his horse and entered the circle.

In a moment, clouds of them were upon him, like a swarm of bees. It felt as if they were sticking pins and needles all over him.

In agony he writhed around; his horse ran off startled.

After the shock and the pain, he remembered his grandfather's advice. He turned his glove inside out and threw it among the Small Folk and before it had reached the ground, they were gone.

But those Small Folk were not done. His horse was gone, and he did not have the faintest idea where he was. He never experienced a darker night. It wasn't until the sun had risen that the enchantment faded and he could see that he was still on the green at the end of Tresidder Lane.

He stood in a dark green circle of grass and something caught his eye. A tiny pair of silver knee buckles of the most ancient shape. They must have fallen off a little gentleman when he had been attacking him.

Mr Trezillian kept the buckles at Tresidder House before they moved to Raftra. They were held as a family prize for a long while, but the Small Folk must have wanted them back because those little buckles have not been seen for a very long time.

TOM KISS-THE-LEEK

Devon

Deep in the library of the Museum of Witchcraft and Magic in Boscastle, I came across Pixy Tales *by Frances Cockerton (1996). I have not been able to trace the story beyond this volume. It is one of my favourites from her collection.*

Tom Bovey was walking home drunk. He wondered how drunk you needed to be to be called drunk, and wondered much drink you needed to have drunk to be classified as a 'drunk'. He was stumbling home from the fair (it had been a gert good evening) and his spirits were high.

He was nearly home when he saw the most incredible vision of a Fairy, tall and thin, impossibly beautiful, dressed in green and standing in a Fairy ring. She waved her arms as he grabbed her and pulled her close.

'You must be a queen,' he said.

It was quite incredible to hold a Fairy. She felt slippery and oh so fragile. He could feel she wanted to slip out of his clumsy fingers. Drunk as he was, he held her gently but refused to let go.

He hurried home, swaying. 'Oh how excited my wife is going to be.'

He knocked over the plant pot and dropped his keys three times, yet, all the while, managed to hold on to the Fairy. Once inside he switched on all the lights and made the most incredible racket climbing the stairs to his bedroom.

'Wife! Wife! Wake up! I've found the most beautiful thing in the world! (Besides you of course.) A Fairy Queen! To bring us luck. Wife!'

He thrust the Fairy in his wife's face.

She had been sleeping, but turned around to regard him with a deadly look.

'You're going to need some luck in the morning,' she said.

He pulled off his braces and used them to strap the Fairy to the bedpost.

She thought him a brute to treat a queen in such a manner. 'Typical,' she thought as she rolled over. Before she had time to close her eyes she could hear Tom snoring heavily beside her.

In the morning he opened his eyes and jumped in shock. There was a leek strapped to the bed frame above his head.

'Wife,' he groaned. 'What is this?'

'Good morning. That's the Fairy Queen you brought home last night, don't you remember? To bring us "luck" you said?'

Tom groaned. He couldn't quite remember what had happened, but he felt suitably embarrassed by the tone of his wife's voice. He unwrapped his braces that held the leek.

He went downstairs, put the kettle on, opened the back door and threw the leek out into the vegetable garden.

Perhaps Tom was still drunk or perhaps his tale was true – it's not for me to say. All I know is that Tom stood there, mouth wide open as the leek turned into the most beautiful Fairy Queen dressed in green. As soon as she stood, a thousand Fairies exploded into being all around her, cheering, 'We've got her back! We've got her back!'

They danced around her and a moment later they all vanished.

Tom ran upstairs and told his wife what he had seen. She groaned at him, but soon enough they were both searching in the garden for the leek, or for signs of a very small Fairy.

While they were searching, the pig got out of its sty and came to help them, unearthing vegetables and causing a new level of chaos upon their morning.

Stories change a little bit every time they are told. But by the time Tom's story was told in the village pub that night, the neighbours decided that the pig had eaten the Fairy and that Tom had kissed the leek.

WHY THE DONKEY IS SAFE

Porlock Wier, Somerset

This wonderful tale was recorded in 1963 by Ruth L. Tongue, who heard it from an old gypsy woman in Worthy Wood above Porlock Weir, Somerset, in 1941.

It is packed full with illuminating folklore:

The cross on the donkey's back is supposed to protect it from witchcraft and seemingly Pixies too.

A child born on Sunday is free from the malice of evil spirits and safe from the effects of overlooking and ill wishing.

And the worldly wisdom that although life might delight your very edges, your mother always knows best.

There was a little, small, young donkey foal born one bright morning and while she was only a few days old, she slipped out of her mammy's sight because she wanted to take a look at life.

She hadn't got far when she met a witch. The witch could clearly see it was a young, unattended donkey and wanted to claim it for her own. So she cast a spell on the donkey to do her bidding.

The spell flew towards the donkey, bounded off her coat and flung straight back at the witch, burning her.

'Yow! Curse you! You were born on a Sunday I don't doubt!'

'Like all dunks, my mammy du say,' said the little, small, young donkey foal, and walked on.

Next, the donkey came across a Bogey.

'I'll 'ave 'ee!' said the Bogey and grabbed the donkey as it was walking by.

But as soon as that Bogey's hands touched the donkey's hair, an electric shock fried the Bogey's fists.

'Yow!' says Bogey, 'Yew gotta criss-cross on your back,' It disappeared into the hedge grumbling, knowing it wouldn't be able to touch her.

'Like all dunks, my mammy du say,' said the little, small, young donkey foal and walked on.

Next the donkey stepped into a gallitrap. A crowd of Pixies leapt into a circle around it ready to claim whatever had walked into their trap. They were sorely disappointed.

'You go on out of our gallitrap!' they said. 'Ere you are, just seven days old, with a criss-cross on your back and we can't touch ee.'

'Like all dunks, my Mammy d' say,' said the little, small, young donkey foal, and walked on.

The donkey returned home, full of the wonders of life. Her mother kicked her for going astray, before giving her dinner.

THREE LITTLE PIXIES

Dartmoor, Devon

We have seen that Pixies like to keep their privacy and hide in plain sight. It is quite appropriate then that this story, which is known by children all over the world, reveals what we thought were pigs are, or were, in Devonshire, Pixies.

The oldest-known published version of 'The Three Little Pigs' features three little Pixies starring in the central role. It appears first in a letter described as 'A Folktale Told on Dartmoor' in the Atheneum Journal, *No. 991, October 1846. The story was submitted to the journal in response to a previously published letter by Ambrose Merton. Merton had written that the stories and traditions of the country were worthy of being recorded and coined the phrase 'folk lore' to describe this study.*

The story was retold in English Forests and Forest Trees *in 1853. Interestingly, a variation of the tale was told by Joel Chandler Harris in* Uncle Remus: His Songs and Sayings, *published in 1881.*

The version with pigs became widely known when Joseph Jacobs included it in English Fairy Tales *in 1890, and it appeared in Andrew Lang's* Green Fairy Book *(1892).*

It's interesting to note that it was common in some areas of Devon to refer to Pixies as 'Pisgies'.

I found it interesting that in a chapter on conjuring in The Fate of the Dead *(1979), Theo Brown notes that within (her) living memory, the circular iron bands from barrels were placed around hen coops on Dartmoor to protect the chickens from foxes. It was thought that foxes cannot pass iron (Brown, 1979, p.56).*

Next time you meet a pig, wonder if it truly is a pig or something else in disguise …

Once upon a time, there was a very hungry fox who was prowling across the high hills of Dartmoor, looking for something delicious to eat. He came upon a hill that was home to a whole host of Pixies. They smelt delicious and he was curious to know what they tasted like.

They were protected in their little Pixie dwellings, but Fox was sly and cunning and knew how to play with his food …

He approached a little house made out of wood and knocked on Pixie's door.

'Let me in!'

'Not a chance!' came Pixie's voice. 'You'll find that my door is fastened.'

Fox leapt on to the wooden structure and scratched and scraped and broke through the roof, landing in Pixie's house and eating Pixie up in an instant.

Fox was pleased. Magic tasted deeeelicious.

Fox had the taste now and wanted more. He followed his nose to another house, this one made of stone.

'Let me in! Let me in!' begged Fox.

'Not on your nelly,' said Pixie inside. 'You'll find that my door is fastened.'

Again Fox leapt on to the roof, dug through the tiles and found his way inside to gobble up the poor Pixie. Delicious!

Fox was hungry for more and next found a house made out of iron.

'Let me in! Let me in! Let me in!'

'No, no! I know what you want!' came Pixie's voice inside. 'You will not come in here tonight.'

Fox leapt on to the roof and tried to destroy the house as he had the previous two. But as hard as he tried, he couldn't get through the iron roof.

Fox returned the next night, knocked on the door and laid on his most foxy charm.

'Good evening, friend. I have just come from the most tempting field of turnips.'

'Turnips?' enquired Pixie.

'Hundreds! I would happily take you there tomorrow. Would 4 a.m. suit you?'

Pixie agreed.

But Pixie outwitted Fox. Pixie found the field and returned home with armfuls of turnips long before Fox had even woken up.

Fox was wild angry when he turned up at 4 a.m. and smelled turnip soup cooking inside the iron-clad home.

'He he he. Thank you, friend,' came the voice inside.

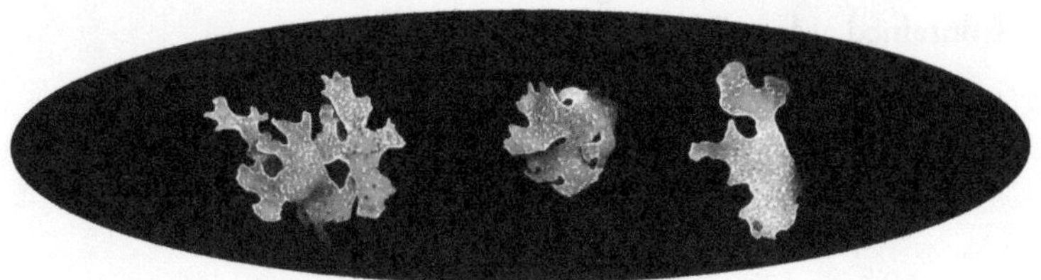

It was a little while before Fox came up with another plan, but he returned.

'Good evening, friend. I wondered if you would like to go to the fair with me tomorrow?'

'The fair?'

'It's not far away, I'd gladly pick you up. Would 3 a.m. suit you?'

Pixie agreed.

Fox came early this time, thinking to surprise Pixie, but he was only up in time to meet Pixie on her way back from the fair. The Pixie had bought a crock, a clock and a frying pan.

When Pixie saw Fox, she leapt into the crock and launched herself down the hill, past Fox and into her iron house.

Again, Fox was furious. But he waited for her to slip up … sooner or later she would let her guard down.

Sure enough, there came a day when Pixie went to bed so tired she forgot to lock the door.

Fox caught Pixie in bed and bundled her into a big chest and locked it quick.

'Ha ha! I have you now, Pixie! Now, how shall I eat you? Raw? Spiced or roasted with turnip?'

'Before you eat me, I must tell you a secret,' said Pixie.

'What kind of secret?'

'A special Pixie secret. It would be such a shame for my magic to die with me.'

'Has the secret got anything to do with where I can find more Pixies?'

'Open the lid, just a crack, and I'll whisper it to you.'

Fox couldn't contain himself; he opened the lid a tiny amount and Pixie whispered an ancient Pixie word – a charm for switching locations. Fox found himself inside his own box as the lid slammed shut, the lock turned and Pixie laughed.

Contained at last, Fox starved to death.

6

TRICK OR TREAT: *S*ECOND *S*IGHT

This book is full of stories of people who have caught glimpses of the Little People. Seeing a chance encounter is a wonder, but the ability to have ongoing psychic perception is another. Second sight is a term used to describe extrasensory perception (ESP), the ability to perceive information beyond the five senses.

In our Pixie-filled region, the most common way of seeing 'beyond the veil' is by using a Fairy ointment. The ointment story (sometimes called 'Fairy Midwife') is a widespread motif across Europe. Versions were made well known by Joseph Jacobs's *English Fairy Tales* (1890) and Andrew Lang's *Lilac Fairy Book* (1910). It is particularly popular in the South West. There are versions associated with Tavistock, Holne, Somerset, Polperro, and various places across West Penwith.

But be warned. When it comes to seeing Pixies and/or Fairies, you should only look upon what you have been given permission to see … or suffer the consequences.

In a variation from the Blackdown Hills of Somerset, a woman received Pixie sight by a moth brushing up against her eye. This enabled her to see the Pixie man who requested her nursing skills to help his wife. (Kruse, *British Pixies*, 2021, p.16)

Anna Eliza Bray documented an early version of the ointment story from Tavistock in 1836. She references Renaissance philosopher and magician Cornelius Agrippa, who gives a recipe for making such an ointment. I spent hours looking through Agrippa's work to find the recipe, but no joy. Then one day in Treadwell's Bookshop in London, I picked up Christina Oakley Harrington's *The Treadwell's*

Book of Plant Magic (2020) and opened it to the page with the recipe I had been seeking.

Sometimes vision is a gift given freely by the Good Folk; other times it is taken without their blessing. Be warned if you see what's not for you.

Note: The story 'Cherry of Zennor' could easily have fitted into this chapter, but as she is a particular example of being spirited away you will find her story under that chapter.

PIXIE BATHWATER

Cornwall

Between 1907 and 1909, American anthropologist Walter Evans-Wentz travelled to the six Celtic regions (Ireland, Scotland, Isle of Man, Wales, Cornwall and Brittany) to record evidence of Fairy experience and encounters. This folk tale was told to him in Cornwall.

There was a woman in Cornwall who was getting a bath ready for her baby. She looked away for just a minute and the Little People dunked their children in first. They were out in a flash, so how was she to know?

The mother washed her child and a droplet of bathwater splashed in her eye. Oh! The world transformed. There were little people everywhere.

One came up to her, 'Can you see our crowd?'

When she said yes, they leapt on her, their fingers reaching to snatch out her eyes. She took her child and ran. They had to clear away as fast as they could.

FAIRIE OINTMENT

Dartmoor, Devon

One of the most vivid storytellers I've ever heard tell is Michael Dacre. In my retelling of this tale I have drawn from his version in Devonshire Folk Tales *(2010) and V. Day Sharman's* Folk Tales of Devon *(1952), which is the version I grew up with.*

Oftentimes the gentleman is described as a Fairy; in various places across the South West he is a Pixy.

Once upon a time there was a midwife who lived in a cottage on the outskirts of Holne on the southern side of Dartmoor. She was highly skilled and much sought after, for doctors were few and far between in those days. Residents of those southern slopes of Dartmoor would visit her for treatments, advice and herbal remedies, but although she helped bring their children into the world, they didn't entirely trust her. The fact was, people believed she was a witch.

Maybe it was because she had a different way of doing things, maybe it was because she wasn't from these parts, but she was definitely different, and she held some power. Maybe they feared her, maybe their religion didn't keep them kinder, maybe they felt inadequate or were just small-minded. Whatever it was, she was tolerated, but not much liked.

'As long as they keep themselves to themselves, I will pay them no heed,' she said to herself as she went about her business. She preferred the company of the trees, the rivers and the stones anyway. She was happy to spend time in the landscape, for the whole world has a story to share if you have attention enough to listen.

Foraging through the Dart valley one day, she heard the cry of the river as the winds changed above her.

'A storm is coming,' she said to herself and turned for home, sensing she should batten down the hatches tonight.

It had grown dark by the time she reached her home, and she had time to make something for dinner before the rain even started to fall.

When the storm really hit, she was nestled safely in bed, comfortable in the fact that there was no chance on earth she would be going out in this weather.

As soon as the thought came to her, a rap, rap, rap came at her door. It was bold and loud and had the sound of authority in every knock.

The lightning started flashing as she got out of bed, her instinct as a midwife overriding her old body's wish to ignore the call and stay in bed.

She opened the door and was startled to see the face of a very wet coal-black horse looking back at her.

'My wife! My wife! You must come now!'

For a wild moment, she thought the horse was talking, but another flash of lighting revealed a small, withered figure in rags standing at her feet. She jumped back when she saw him.

He was one of the Good Folk, ancient as an oak root, with a rather terrifying look in his eye. She usually kept a safe distance from the Pixies.

'You must attend to my wife. She is having a child and needs your help straight away!' His voice was as shrill as a thrush as he spoke.

She feared getting involved with the Good Folk; they were tricksy characters.

'You must be mad, the night is so awful. I wouldn't leave the house tonight for the King of England himself!' she said firmly and went to close the door.

'What about the King of Pixieland? Please! You will not be harmed,' assured the little man. 'You will be compensated for your troubles. Twenty gold coins. Half now, half on completion.'

The Pixie withdrew a money bag from the horse and passed it to the lady.

It was more than she made in five years! It was worth the risk of it turning to leaves, because if it didn't …

'I'll get my coat and tools.'

Moments later, she was out in the wind and the rain, sitting on the horse, ready to go.

'For your own protection, you will need to be blindfolded,' he said, tying a green cloth over her eyes. She didn't like it, but accepted the condition.

He mounted the horse and off they went, faster than the wind around the tors. She tried to imagine which path took them into the Faerie realm, but they journeyed so rapidly, on and on, up and over, she could barely keep up. She imagined they could have crossed the moor several times over, before they finally came to a stop.

He helped her down from the horse and hurried her out of the storm. He led her to what she imagined was a building. She heard a lock click and a door open, and when inside they were finally sheltered from the wind and rain. Her feet echoed along a stone passageway.

'You can take off the blindfold now,' he said, revealing a simple cottage room. A tiny woman lay on a small bed, panting heavily with child.

She didn't think it looked like the home of the King of the Pixies, but she knew Pixies were tricksy. They would say anything to get her to help.

'Young ones are rare with us now, so, I beg you, please do all you can to save them both,' the Pixie gentleman pleaded.

While the storm raged on, the midwife set to work, and after a long while, a baby was born.

It squealed, ear-shatteringly loud, which made its crumpled face and pointy ears rather hard to look at kindly.

The Pixie gentleman came back into the room to see his wife and meet his child. A light shone through his face with joy and relief.

Seeing the midwife in discomfort at the babe's screeching, he smiled and gave her a small jar of green ointment.

'Perhaps you should do the honours. Dab this on the babe's eyelids and it will calm,' he said gently. 'But be careful, keep it away from your eyes, this is not safe for humans.'

She did as she was told and instantly the child was silenced, and peace fell upon the room. The midwife let out a huge sigh of relief and while the family embraced, she looked at the ointment, wondering what ingredients made something so potent. An ointment like this would be incredibly useful for her.

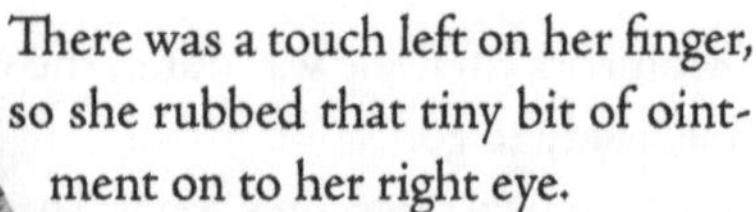

There was a touch left on her finger, so she rubbed that tiny bit of ointment on to her right eye.

It stung for a moment as a bright vision took over her. She could see two images overlayed in her vision. Closing her left eye, a hidden world was revealed by her right eye.

What had been a cottage before was now a vast chambered bedroom. The mother was no longer tiny, but human size, as regal as a queen dressed in white and gold. The walls glittered, decorated with living patterns of translucent wings, bathed in primrose light.

The room was full of attendants, seeing to the mother and child. They seemed oblivious to her.

The withered Pixy gentleman was now as tall as a man and as handsome as a prince. His rags were now velvet and he smiled as he came towards her. Truly, he was a king. 'Here is the second part of your payment, with our thanks,' he said with a smile.

Discreetly as she could, the midwife concealed her astonishment and covered her right eye. Suddenly all reverted to how it had been, moments before.

'Thank you for all you have done for us this evening,' said the man, small once again.

'I will take you home whenever you are ready.'

'Better sooner than later,' she said with a tired smile.

On went the blindfold and on they both went on the back of the horse. The storm had finished, and it seemed that they arrived back in the familiar hills of Holne in no time at all.

'Goodbye, nurse! Goodbye! We will be in your debt forever,' he called against the wind as he rode off into the dark night.

She was relieved to be home, and went wearily to bed.

It was late into the morning when the midwife rose, her cat clawing at her bed, demanding breakfast.

She opened her right eye and got the fright of her life. Her cat was huge, larger than a panther, and as a regal as an Egyptian sphinx. She bolted up in bed and covered her right eye, and the magical vision flickered away.

'Miaw,' called her normal-sized cat, impatiently.

She went into the kitchen and checked the Pixy payment – twenty gold pieces! It had not turned to leaves.

Covering her left eye, she looked around. She knew instinctively that her wooden table had come from a tree that knew the songs of the stars. The teacups tinkled on her dresser – each one had a little spirit playing inside them. She closed her right eye and normality returned to her kitchen.

The midwife decided that she'd treat herself and take the horse down to Ashburton to buy herself a new dress and a cupboard full of food.

As she rode, she wondered at the world through her right eye. Nature was so very alive. Stones murmured their songs, insects spoke in riddles and mathematic equations, the trees gossiped with their neighbours, each leaf seemed to have an opinion, and every blade of grass was full of things to say. Soon she could no longer bear it, it was overwhelming.

Ashburton was full of people for market day, and she gazed, amazed at the visions she saw through her magical eye. There were people of all sizes, taller and shorter than the humans around her, who disappeared when she closed that right eye.

People wore their thoughts on their faces, and she saw their feelings dart in shapes and colours around them.

One person looked like they were raining as they walked past her.

She made her way through the market and saw the Pixy gentleman through her right eye. He was as tall as a man, and she watched as he picked up an orange and walked off without paying for it.

She followed him and said, 'Tut tut, good sir. I saw that. Now, how is your lady and baby doing this morning?'

His face was shocked with alarm and dropped into sadness when he saw her.

'Which eye can you see me out of?' He said coming towards her.

'Erm … w-with the r-right eye …'

'I am sorry to do this, for you have done good by us, but there is nothing else to be done.'

He touched her right eye so gently, but a sharp feeling of grit underneath her eyelid made her wince, and when she opened it finally, the magical sight and the man had disappeared. It hurt to see, and before long she saw nothing else from her right eye.

She was blind in her right eye for the rest of her life. However, she never stopped feeling how alive the world was, and although she couldn't see it, she found new ways to listen, to speak and to see.

ANN JEFFERIES

St Teath, Cornwall

For the next story we must travel along the north coast of Cornwall, between Port Isaac and Camelford to the little village of St Teath.

In a document held in Exeter, dated 1345, St Teath (pronounced like 'death', not 'teeth') is listed as a destination pilgrims might be interested in travelling to in order to lessen their time in purgatory.

To start the story of Ann Jefferies, we must visit St Teath in the mid-seventeenth century. At this time Britain was in a period of rebellion and political insecurity. Across the British Isles, the English Civil Wars (1642–51) were being fought between the Parliamentarians and the Royalists. Cornwall's Pendennis Castle held the last Royalist stronghold on the mainland, but in 1646 King Charles I surrendered, resulting in his execution (1649). During this period of volatility, the mania of the witch trials grew to a terrible peak.

Among the wars of men, Atlantic waves ever crash along Cornwall's rugged coast and the stitchwort flowers ever bloom.

Jefferies (1625–1713) was a real woman who lived in St Teath. She started seeing Fairies when she was around 19 years old. Not only did she repeatedly have Fairy encounters, but she gained various powers from them, enabling her to heal wounds and ailments by touch, predict the future and even inflict harm on others.

There are various 'folk tale' stories of Ann, but as she and her tale are quite so extraordinary, I have worked from the original source recording the case: a letter Moses Pitt wrote to the Bishop of Gloucester in 1696.

It is important to note that Ann did not want her story told. She did not want to kick up more trouble in her later years. Here we are, nearly 400 years later, and Ann's story is a unique historical document of an incredible woman.

I have wondered long and hard how best to honour Ann's story. I hope this telling does her justice.

'Will you tell us your story, Ann?' Humphrey asked the lady, who had turned away from him, staring out of the window on this rainy day. Seventy years of life might have aged her, but she kept her secrets as firm as an oak. 'You know my uncle has commissioned this interview?'

'Yes, yes. You have read me Mr Pitt's letter. He has been wanting the same thing these past five years. My answer remains no.'

Why was she so obstinate? Had she not known him all her life? Could she not trust him?

As if she could read his mind, she turned to face him, making him jump.

'I'll tell you for why. You'll send my words to our dear publisher, Moses Pitt. He'll write my life into a book or a ballad or something equally dreadful. I shall not have *my* name spread around the country in such a manner, even if I had five hundred pounds for the pleasure.'

'But yours is an incredible life Ann! It should be remembered and told. Your story is extraordinary.'

There was a long pause.

'Not even if my dear old Pa came back from the dead would I discover him the things that happened to me back then.'

Mr Humphrey Martyn waited, hoping to convince her otherwise. He was expecting her to be hard work, but she refused to budge an inch.

'But ...'

'Humphrey, I have been questioned before justices, in prison, by Tregeagle himself. If my story is known more publicly, I shall be sought out again, and given no peace. I do not consent to this interview.'

Finally, he admitted defeat.

'Thank you for your time Ann.'

He closed the door behind him. Ann turned to look out the window with a hard stare, as raindrops danced down the glass.

In his London home, Moses Pitt received Humphrey's disappointing letter.

'Well, I may have been 7 years old when all this happened, but I was there too.' He got out his paper and ink. 'I will tell the story of Ann Jefferies.'

Ann Jefferies was born to a poor family in the Parish of St Teath, Cornwall, in 1625. It was custom at the time for the most affluent to take on the poorest in their communities as apprentices, to work for food and board. So it came to be that Ann was brought into the home of Mary Martyn.

The year is 1645 and Ann is 19 years old. She has been in the house for numerous years and is well liked. She is bold and would venture at difficulties that boys would think twice about.

Ann was knitting in the arbour when all of a sudden six Little People clothed in green came over the hedge upon her.

So frightened was she, she fell into a convulsive fit. Mary found her in this condition and brought her inside, greatly worried for the poor girl. They put her in bed, at which point she recovered long enough to look Mary right in the eyes and say 'Little People! They are going out of the window. Do you not see them?'

Mary believed the girl was delusional and settled Ann to rest.

Ann remained in sickness for a long time, crying out with eagerness, distemper, frailty. She could not be roused out of bed, so when Mary's mother-in-law died, she dared not tell Ann unless it should make her condition worse. Ann's distemper continued so long it was wondered whether she had become a changeling.

As she began to recover, they could see she was different. If angered, she would fall into her fits and they continued endlessly. The family were afraid she might die in one of them.

When she recovered enough strength to go to church, she paid her devotions to God. She took delight in this, and although she could not read, she loved hearing the word of her God spoken aloud.

Ann's unpredictability weighed on the family, especially Mary.

One harvest day, when all of the family were in the fields and Mary's boy Moses was at school, Mary and Ann were alone in the house. Mary needed to retrieve some meal from the mill. Not being able to trust Ann with the task or be left alone in the house, Mary decided she would go to the mill herself, which was only a quarter of a mile from the house.

Mary asked Ann if she would like to wait in the garden while she went to the mill.

Ann declined.

'I don't trust you in the house alone. Please go outside,' said Mary.

'I don't want to.'

'It is not a matter for debate, Ann. You can hardly help yourself, you'll be a mischief if anything happens while I am away.'

Mary took Ann by the arm and led her outside so she could lock the front door behind her. Ann waited in the orchard until Mary returned. But although the mill was so close, Mary did not return.

On leaving the mill, Mary had slipped, hurting her leg so badly that she could not get up.

She lay there in great pain for hours, until a neighbour on horseback came across her and brought her back home.

As soon as she was at the house, she sent word to retrieve the servants in the fields, for Mary could not manage anything, especially Ann, in this state.

Soon the house was full of people. It was decided a rider should be sent the 8 miles to Bodmin to fetch the surgeon. It would be expensive, but Mary was in a bad way. While the horse was being made ready, Ann approached Mary.

'I'm sorry you fell, Mary. I suspect you slipped by that large stone where the fern grows darkest?'

Mary looked at Ann. 'How could you possibly know that?'

'Can I see the damaged leg?' asked Ann.

Annoyed, Mary refused the girl, 'What good will it do?'

Ann was persistent to the point of annoyance, so Mary allowed the silly girl to see her leg.

Ann started to stroke it with her hand.

'Does that feel better?' asked Ann.

Mary confessed that, indeed, it did.

Ann suggested to call off sending for the surgeon.

'Well, I'm not sure …'

Ann stroked the leg a little more and helped Mary to stand.

'It's extraordinary, Ann. It doesn't hurt at all!' exclaimed Mary, 'But how did you do it? And how did you know where I fell? I have not told anyone of it.'

Ann looked down, 'Half a dozen Little People told me.'

Mary said it wasn't possible.

'It is,' said Ann. 'I was vexed at you something rotten for bringing me outside this morning, when I didn't want to be, and … the Little People returned.'

Mary looked concerned, but Ann went on.

'They come to me often, Mary, they are the same ones who came the day I had my first fit … Let me tell you the truth of it.' For the first time, Ann spoke about what had been happening to her.

'That very first time they came, I had been darning socks in the arbour and they frightened the life out of me. That was when my sickness began. Six Little People, all in green, jumped out of the hedge, upon me all of a sudden. They have been visiting, ever since, talking with me, playing with me. Curiously, they only ever appear in even numbers, of two, four, six or eight. They follow me and talk to me and jump out of the window whenever they leave.

'When I was angered all alone earlier today, they returned. They asked me if I was outside against my will. I told them I was. "Well," they said, "Mary will not fare better for it," and they told me that you would fall, and the exact place where it would be.'

Mary realised she was suddenly a bit frightened of Ann.

'But, they told me they would give me the power to cure your leg, and a surgeon wouldn't be needed.'

The cure of Mary's leg was as astonishing as it was complete. Mary did not need the surgeon. The miraculous healing girl made a noise all throughout the county and people started visiting the house to be healed by Ann. They started coming from Land's End, and soon enough they were coming from London.

Ann never accepted coins from any of the visitors. 'Why should I charge for what was given to me for free?'

She never spent time making salves or ointments; she healed people by the lightest touch.

The neighbours in St Teath were fascinated with Ann. Whispers circulated that she could turn invisible, and they often caught Ann dancing among the orchard's trees. When asked if she was well, she would reply, 'I'm dancing with the Fairies!'

She became known as a healer and as a seer. She received prophecies and visions of people who were on the way to the house. She announced their arrival, sometimes several days before they would arrive, so the household was always well prepared.

As time drew on, Ann dealt more with the Fairies than she did with humans, and she spent more time withdrawn. If she received a prophecy, she would tell the family, then retreat into her rooms and not talk for days. One day she stopped eating food and declared that she would depend on the Good Folk to bring her sustenance.

Amazingly, Ann survived on Fairy bread, forsaking human food for six months, except on Christmas day, when she ate beef with the family.

The news that a cunning lady was being fed by Faeries upset the magistrates and ministers enough that they decided to visit the household.

She gave them rational answers to all their questions, which must have disappointed them. The ministers endeavoured to persuade her that she dealt with evil spirits, delusions sent by the devil.

Ann asked them how could that be when they did no hurt, and indeed they helped cure anyone who came to her?

The ministers were unmoved and when they left, the family suggested it might be better to give the communication with the Fairies a rest for a while.

Ann looked at them and said, 'But even now they call me.'

The family pleaded her not to go.

'They are calling me a second time.'

Still she did not go.

'They are calling me a third time.'

This time she got up and went to her room to speak with them.

After she had been with them for some time, she came downstairs with the Bible in her hand. She told the family that the Fairies had asked her to read the 1st Epistle of St John, Chapter 4, Verse 1 …'

Ann could not read, so she passed the Bible to Mary, who read aloud, 'Dearly beloved, believe not every spirit, but try the spirits whether they be of God.'

Early in the new year of 1647, Ann was milking the cow when the Fairies appeared and told her that a constable was on his way to arrest her. Ann asked if she should hide herself. They answered, 'No. Fear nothing, go with the constable, take your Bible, we will be with you.'

The constable arrived with a warrant from John Tregeagle himself, Steward to John, Earl of Radnor, the Justice of the Peace in Cornwall. Ann was sent to Bodmin gaol, where she was imprisoned for three months. Ann was not treated kindly, and because she told them that Fairies brought her food, she was starved for the duration of the stay. She did not complain; the Fairies found their way to bring her food to survive.

She was coherent and compliant, and surprised all who questioned her with her knowledge of the Bible. She was a tough case to crack.

'You are a dangerous character and you spread lies,' accused Tregeagle.

'Did you not say, "The King shall return to the throne, taking revenge upon his enemies?"'

She confirmed she had.

After three months Ann was released, but Tregeagle was hungry for blood and imprisoned her in a gaol at his own home for a few months more. He continually starved her, but the Fairies kept her alive.

At last she found her freedom, but was ordered by the Justice of Peace that she was not to return to the house of Mary where she had become one of the family. She was relocated to the home of Mary's sister-in-law in Padstow. She smiled and nodded when she heard that the King had returned to the throne, the Fairies were always right

She married and continued helping people locally with their ailments until her old age.

'That will do it,' thought Moses at his desk in London, when he had finished writing Ann's story, 'That will do it.'

Somewhere in Cornwall, six little spirits danced through a rain-soaked window and up to a troubled Ann. They whispered in her ear and her furrowed brow relaxed, and she smiled.

THE FOUR-LEAF CLOVER

West Penwith, Cornwall

Both Bottrell and Hunt record this story, and attribute the tale to two neighbouring farms near St Buryan. I have visited both farms, and when passing through was delighted to find two gnome statues leaning against the barn at Bosfranken. I have drawn from both of their versions, but in honour of the gnomes have worked mostly from Hunt's.

Daisy was a beautiful shorthorn cow, totally red on one side and red and white on the other. Her udders were always full and her dewlaps would brush the flowering grasses as she grazed through the fields.

In any field she was clearly the farmer's prize cow, but there was something very curious about Daisy. As much as she was milked, she was never milked to empty. The milkmaid could fill a bucket full to the brim, but while there was visibly another 2 gallons in her udder, Daisy would bleat and cock up her head and the milk flow would stop.

Try as the milkmaid would, no more milk would yield. At first, the farmer thought it was his milkmaid who was the problem, but whomever on the farm tried to milk Daisy, they all found the same thing.

'She's ill-wished, it must be an enchantment,' the farmer and his wife agreed. Well, they mostly agreed because it didn't truly make sense. Daisy was so healthy and so very fat, these were not the usual signs of an ill-wished cow.

If anything, she was blessed! She produced milk all seasons, even throughout winter.

It was curious for sure.

One spring the farmer decided it was better luck to take her to market than to risk an enchanted cow on his farm. She would easily fetch the best price in his herd.

So, one morning in May, they led Daisy away from the farm at Bosfranken, up to St Buryan to market. But as they drove her up Alsia lane, she broke free and charged down the lane towards Crean. She ran along the footpath that crossed the fields back to Bosfranken. As if she knew the quickest way, she walked straight through a hedge that got her back into the field they had just taken her from. She did not want to go to market.

'Very curious indeed!' said the farmer.

That midsummer's day, the maid was milking Daisy in the field and, sure enough, once the bucket was full, Daisy stopped full flow and refused to give any more.

The bucket was so full she could scarcely lift the thing to balance it on her head.

So she grabbed a handful of grass to place on her hat, to soften the weight and steady the bucket.

But as soon as she put the grass on her head, she saw the most extraordinary sight.

There were hundreds, possibly thousands, of Little Folk in the field all around, swarming around Daisy. Daisy's milk was in full flow and the Little People were collecting it.

Some held foxglove flower cups, Lady's smocks and buttercups, which they held up to collect the showering of milk, each standing on tiptoe on the grasses and clover flowers beneath Daisy's udder. Even with their flowers full to the brim, the spirits didn't seem to bear any weight beneath them.

One little character was bigger than the rest and clung to the underside of Daisy's belly. It had a straw in its mouth, which it lowered into the little cups that were filling below. It drank up all the milk that had been collected until the little person below realised it had been tricked and had to wait for a refill.

'You must be a Piskey,' thought the milkmaid as she watched it laugh and laugh each time it emptied another flower cup.

More spirits came, riding hares, which they left in the field, and hurried towards Daisy to get some milk for themselves.

It looked like there was a whole midsummer festival around Daisy. Little Folk were scratching and tickling between her horns; they stroked and combed her hair; they twisted off ticks that had dug into her flesh and they whispered their stories into her ears. Daisy smiled as she chewed on fresh grass.

'No wonder her hair is always so shiny and in place,' thought the girl, who wasn't totally shocked to see the spirits. Somehow it all made total sense to her.

Suspecting her milkmaid was slacking off, the farmer's wife called from the gate, 'What's taking so long then?'

All the spirits looked towards the mistress and, with a rather distasteful look in their eyes, vanished.

When the maid told what she had seen, to her surprise the mistress believed her. 'You must have a four-leaf clover on you, girl.'

They looked through the grasses she had put on her head and sure enough there was a four-leaf clover among them.

'So that's where all our extra milk is going,' said the farmer when his wife told him what she had learned. 'Best you visit your old mother to find out how we scare them away.'

The mistress's mother was old Betty, a fine old dame who lived in St Buryan. She knew the country ways and how to deal with witches and Fairies and such things.

She visited old Betty the next day, who told her, 'Those Little People can't abide the smell of fish, nor salt or grease. Rub the udder with fish brine and see if you won't frighten the Little People away.'

She did exactly what old Betty had said, and it turns out she was quite right, but she regretted it every day after.

Daisy did indeed give them all the milk she produced, but she didn't produce as much as she had. All day the cow would walk sorrowfully through the fields, bleating and crying as if she had lost her calf. As she pined away, her rich coat grew dull and she withered away to skin and bone.

She was taken to market, but was sold for next to nothing.

I don't know what became of Daisy, but nothing thrived on that farm for the farmer and his wife for a long time after that.

7

SPIRITED AWAY: INTO THE OTHERWORLD

See saw;
Margery Daw,
Sold her bed
and lay upon straw;
She sold her straw,
and lay upon hay,
So Piskies came
And carried her away.

This Cornish version of the well-known nursery rhyme is a curiosity. It seems to suggest Margery has fallen on repeated hard times (possibly self-inflicted?) until she is stolen away by the Piskies. Whoever she was, the lesson is clear … Watch yourself, or the Piskies might carry you away.

Changelings are fairytale characters that have terrified parents and children across Europe for generations. The idea is that a human child is stolen by the Fairies and swapped with a sickly/deceased Fairy replacement. Depending where the story is from, there are local responses, such as harming the changeling in specific ways, or treating it kindly to convince the abductor that they should swap it back.

Sometimes the healthy child is returned, other times the changeling dies and the baby is never seen again. Sometimes the child recovers for a period, but is forever changed by the experience and dies early.

It is not only babies who are stolen away. Sometimes, adults (usually female) can be taken into the otherworld to care for a Fairy child, or to act as servant for a certain period of time/eternally.

It is very probable many Changeling stories originated from some form of lived experience so it is interesting to see how their tales have evolved. 'The Lost Child of St Allen' has been repeatedly documented since mid seventeenth century, in latter years it has been portrayed as an enchanted encounter rather than a traumatic incident. I can't help but think that these stories might reveal how generations have held and met fears, traumas and collective grief.

In this chapter, we will see various ways in which one might be spirited away, beyond the veil into the other world. All of these stories come from Cornwall, although there was belief in changelings and tales in Devon and Somerset, too. Indeed, Bray records Devon mothers pinning children to their clothes as a precaution against Fairy kidnappers in 1836.

CHERRY OF ZENNOR

West Penwith, Cornwall

Zennor is a small village on the north coast of West Penwith, between St Ives and St Just. It is home to many folk tales and legends, old and recent. It is also famously home to the Mermaid of Zennor.

Inland the high hills of the Lady Downs are marked by traces of our Neolithic ancestors. Zennor Quoit is a ruined but impressive burial chamber that dates back to the Bronze Age. Originally thought to have been covered by an earth mound 'barrow' 13 metres wide, the stone structure now lays exposed.

A short walk away is the abandoned house where, in the 1930s, notorious occultist Aleister Crowley is said to have summoned the devil, resulting in the death of neighbouring resident Ka Cox.

A long, long time ago, on the windswept cliffside of Treen, near Zennor, there was a two-bedroom cottage. Here Old Honey lived with his wife and ten children. You can imagine, with twelve mouths to feed, they never had much money but they worked hard and grew what they could.

While the older siblings went fishing, the younger ones spent their days collecting 'crogans' (limpets) and 'gweans' (periwinkles) down by the beach. By the heaps of shells strung on strings outside that little cottage, you might imagine they ate nothing else. But they also had potatoes and fish, and even had pork some Sundays.

Their eldest was Cherry. She was wild as the skies, mischievous as the wind and could run as fast as a hare. Whenever the miller's boy visited the house to see if Old Honey wanted to send some corn to the mill, Cherry would untie his horse and ride it up the cliffs. The miller's boy would catch up eventually, out of breath, and they would laugh as they returned home.

As she grew into a teenager, Cherry became discontented.

Her friends always had new dresses for Morvah Fair, but she only ever had the same worn-out thing to wear. Year after year, her mother kept promising her a new dress, but the money was always 'too tight' when it came to it. 'Maybe next year.'

She stopped going to fair, to church, or to town. She couldn't bear to be seen in the rags she had mended again and again.

Cherry's heart sank as she missed the fair the year she turned 16. Her friends came to tell her about it with new ribbons in their hair, new dresses and the stories of the boys who had flirted with them.

That night a frustration boiled inside Cherry; she had outgrown her dress, her cottage, her family.

'Mother! I can't eat another sodding limpet! I can't stay here in these rags all my life, it's time for me to leave, find work and make my own way. I will return when I have afforded myself a new dress and not before.'

'Darling Cherry, we will miss you, but I understand. I only ask you don't go further than Towednack. Then we can see you now and again on a Sunday.'

'No, no!' said Cherry. 'I've got to go further than that. I don't want to settle for a place where the most interesting thing to happen was when the cows ate the bellringer's rope. I want more civilised folk. Perhaps I'll make it to Truro.'

Her mother whimpered and had to sit down at the thought.

The next morning, Cherry said goodbye to her mother and father and her sorrow-filled siblings.

Her father wished her well. 'Mind you, be careful of sailors, robbers and pirates.'

She promised her parents she would try to find work as close to home as she could, and come home at the earliest opportunity.

She hardly looked back as she took the path to Ludgvan that would lead her out of the moors towards Penzance.

The moment she lost sight of the chimneys of Treen, she turned and suddenly felt a surprise change of heart. A strange feeling grew in her. It was the first time she had felt alone. Ever more determined, she went on.

She climbed up into the hills and eventually came to the crossroads on the Lady Downs. The moors felt barren and huge. She couldn't see a soul for miles in any direction. The feeling of loneliness made her feel small and powerless.

There was a large stone by the roadside. She sat and without warning she wept for the home she was leaving and the family she loved. She wondered when she would see them again.

The tears made her wonder if she was making a mistake. She could easily turn around and make the best of living at home. Maybe she could marry the miller's boy and be happy.

She wiped her tears and held up her head, and was surprised to see a gentleman walking towards her. She wondered where he could possibly have come from.

'Good morning,' said the gentleman. He enquired about the road to Towdenack and asked Cherry where she was going.

'I'm from Zennor, sir. I left home this morning to look for work, but it seems my heart is failing me. I think it's best I return home.'

'Well, well! I never expected to meet with such luck! I don't live far, and I have just set out to seek a nice clean girl to help keep house. And here you are.'

He told Cherry that he had recently become a widower and needed someone to care for his dear boy and keep the house. 'You're just the girl to do it.'

Cherry brightened, this felt fortuitous indeed. The gentleman spoke smoothly and was in such fine attire.

'Is this your work?' he said, pointing out a patch on her dress that she had re-sewn several times. She flushed red.

'What excellent work, it's almost seamless. I really do believe you would be perfect if you would consider it? You're as sweet as a rose and all the water in the sea would not make you cleaner.'

Cherry blushed. She wasn't much used to flattery or to talking with a gentleman. If she was honest, she didn't quite understand everything he said. But her mother had taught her to be proper and say, 'Yes, sir' to the parson or any gentleman even if she didn't understand what they had to say. So that's what she did.

The gentleman told her he lived a short way away, just off the moor in the low countries. 'You would have very little to do every day. Have you ever milked a cow?'

Cherry brightened and agreed to go with him.

He talked so kindly and was always one step ahead, so that Cherry lost all notion of time or how far they had walked.

Soon, they were in lanes so green with trees she could barely see a postage stamp of sky. The path was thick with grasses and flowers, roots and earth. Sweetbriars and honeysuckles perfumed the air, and the reddest ripe apples hung out on branches across the lane.

This was nothing like windy Zennor. She marvelled at the abundant beauty of it all when suddenly they arrived at a stream of crystal-clear water crossing their path. Cherry wondered how best to cross. That moment the gentleman put his arm under hers and lifted her ever so gently, and for the briefest moment it seemed that they glided through the air before landing on the side.

The trees grew thicker and thicker and the path darker and darker as it got narrower and narrower. They descended the hill. Cherry held on to the man's arm and thought herself so very lucky to have found such a fine gentleman. She felt she could go to the world's end with him.

After walking a little more, the gentleman revealed a hidden gate in the lane, which opened out into the most gorgeous garden. 'Cherry, my dear, this is where we live.'

Cherry could scarcely believe her eyes. It was the most beautiful place she had ever seen. Bushes of colours, in hues she had no name for, grew verdantly everywhere. There was such depth to the garden that she could see through gaps between the colourful trees into further reaches of the garden, where more colours shone.

Fruits hung above her of varieties she could not name, butterflies and bees fluttered and darted, and the birdsong! It was as if the chorus of birdsong sang in unison to celebrate the sweetness of this place.

Her grannie had told her of enchanted places – was this one of them? She looked for a moment at the gentleman who was leading her on a pathway towards the house. He couldn't be one of the Good Folk. He was as big as a priest.

A little boy came running up to them, 'Papa! Papa!'

The child seemed to be about 2 or 3 years old, but there was something knowing in his eyes. They were brilliant, piercing eyes, with an expression so crafty. Cherry's eyes darted to her feet to avoid looking at him.

Looking up, she saw an old lady hurrying towards them after the boy. Her face was angry and twisted. She shot Cherry a dangerous look, grabbed the boy by the arm and dragged him back to the house without a word of welcome.

The master explained that the woman was Aunt Prudence, his late wife's grandmother, and she would be leaving this place as soon as Cherry knew her work. 'She's a terrible bore – truth be told I can't stand having her,' he whispered in her ear.

Cherry relaxed a little as he led her around a yew tree from where she could see a grand house. 'Welcome to my home,' he said, taking her inside.

The house was as green as the garden. Vases and pots filled with plants and flowers decorated the sideboards and trailed from stands. Plants everywhere, and the sun seemed to shine within the walls, although she could not see how.

'After supper Aunt Prudence will instruct you on everything you will need to know,' said the master. Dinner was ready extraordinarily fast and was a feast. There were foods Cherry had never eaten before, and tastes that shocked and delighted her. She didn't dare show her ignorance by asking what they were.

After supper Aunt Prudence directed her to a room at the top of the house, where she and the child were to sleep.

'That's your bed, and you better keep your eyes closed whether you're asleep or not, lest you see something you'd rather not see,' said Aunt Prudence strictly, 'And don't you dare speak to the child!'

Cherry was instructed to rise at the break of day and take the child to the spring in the garden and wash him in the pool. Hidden in a cleft in the rock, she would find a crystal box with some ointment. After the child was bathed, she should anoint his eyes with it, 'But whatever you do, you are not, on any account, to touch it to your own eyes.'

There was a long silence

'And then, what should I do?'

'Well, put it back of course,' shrilled Prudence. 'Then you are to call the cow, fill a bucket for the house, and draw a bowl for the boy's breakfast.'

Aunt Prudence left her, only to return a few moments later with the boy.

Cherry was dying with curiosity by now, so as they readied for bed, she tried asking him questions. Glee erupted on the boy's face, 'You're not meant to talk to me. I'll tell Aunt Prue!' Cherry drew silent.

The next morning she did as she was charged. Waking at sunrise, she took the boy downstairs and found the milk bucket, and into the garden they went to find the spring. The water poured crystal clear from a granite rock into a gorgeous pool. The stones were covered in moss and overhanging fern decorated it beautifully. After the boy was washed she remembered the ointment, which she found, hidden away, just as she was told it would be. She opened it to reveal an ointment as green as clover, which she applied to the boy's eyes.

Cherry looked around for the cow, but saw nothing. The boy laughed, 'You have to call her.'

'Pruit! Pruit! Pruit!' was how she called the cows at home and obediently the most beautiful cow walked between the trees and stood on the bank beside Cherry.

Cherry brought the bucket under the cow's udder and as soon as she touched a teat four streams of milk poured into the bucket, filling it in seconds. Cherry was nearly knocked off her feet!

The boy laughed and laughed as Cherry put his breakfast bowl under the streaming teats.

He drank the milk as quickly as it was filled.

The cow was satisfied that its job had been done well and walked off between the trees with a satisfied 'moo'.

They returned to the house, where breakfast was waiting. As they ate, Aunt Prudence told Cherry the daily tasks.

'Scald the milk, make the butter, wash all the plates and platters, cups and bowls ...

'Keep to the kitchen, you'll have plenty to do. Avoid curiosity, Don't bother the master. There are parts of the house that you are not welcome in, so if a door is locked it is not for you.'

Cherry nodded obediently 'Yes, mam.'

After her tasks had been finished that day, her master required Cherry's help in the garden. They filled baskets with ripe apples and pears, and she spent time weeding the leeks and onions.

Cherry loved being in the garden, especially with her master, and away from the watchful gaze of Aunt Prudence.

Though she was never far away. Aunt Prudence brought the child and her knitting into the garden and, even when occupied by both, she still managed to keep an eye on Cherry.

Cherry heard her grumbling, 'I knew Robin would find some fool from Zennor, but it would be better for both if she had stayed away.'

Cherry loved the company of her master. She loved being in the garden too, and when she finished a task for him sometimes he would give her a kiss on the cheek.

One day, Aunt Prudence told Cherry she needed her in a different part of the house. 'Bring the beeswax and a cloth!'

Aunt Prudence led Cherry down a long, dark passage. 'Take off your shoes, girl,' said Aunt Prudence as she unlocked a door. They entered a room where the floor was shiny as glass.

Cherry paused. It was an extraordinary room, filled with statues and figures on shelves, recesses and plinths. Figures of all kinds of people circled the room, tall and small. Some were missing their heads, legs or arms. Cherry felt like they might come to life at any moment.

She placed one foot on the glassy floor but if felt like she was stepping underground, like she was turning upside down, like all the blood was rushing to her head. 'I don't want to go any further,' Cherry pleaded.

'Come, now!'

Cherry took a deep breath and followed Aunt Prudence up to a long, thin box, standing on six legs in the centre of the room. Old Prudence laughed, 'Come now, all I need from you is just a bit of polishing my dear! Polish this box 'til you can see your face in it.'

Cherry felt sick – it looked like a coffin on legs. 'Rub, girl!'

Finding her courage, Cherry polished the box while Aunt Prudence laughed, 'Rub! Rub! Rub! Faster, girl! Harder and faster!' laughed Aunt Prudence.

Cherry whimpered and shook as she polished the box, until, desperately, she pushed it too hard and the box wobbled.

An unearthly, doleful bellow erupted from the box. Cherry fell to the ground, paralysed with fear, thinking all the statues were approaching her.

The master stormed into the room, silencing the earth-shattering dread. He picked up Cherry, who had fainted, and took her out of the room.

Furious with Prudence for taking her into the locked room, he kicked her out of the house and took Cherry to the kitchens to give her a drink of cordial.

The drink calmed her senses and erased her memory of the events, but it could not remove that feeling of dread. There was something fearful behind those locked doors.

But now Aunt Prudence was gone, Cherry was mistress of the house. She took on the duties of the household and enjoyed being in charge. Sometimes the master was away for weeks at a time, and those times felt long and sad. She liked it best when he was with her.

Every day she collected endless ripe fruit and picked flowers from the garden to fill the house.

When he was home, the master began to spend more and more time in the shut-up apartments. When Cherry drew near to that corridor she feared, she could hear many voices coming from beyond the locked door.

As the sun rose one morning, and she was washing the boy in the spring, Cherry realised she had everything she could possibly want, but still wasn't happy.

She knew there was more to this place than she was seeing.

Even the child, with his sharp strange eyes, seemed to see more than she did.

She put the ointment on to his eyes and watched them flash brighter.

What was this stuff?

She milked the cow and fed the child who, as usual, ran off without so much as a thank you. Instead of returning to the house, she went back to the spring, to the crystal box with the ointment.

With the smallest amount on her finger, she dabbed a touch on her eyelid.

It hurt as if she had thrust a burning stick into her eye. She screamed and fell to her knees. She plunged her face into the spring for relief.

She opened her eyes and the pain subsided. To her great surprise, the pool was filled with tiny Little People! Hundreds of them, mostly ladies singing, dancing and laughing. At the bottom of the spring pool there was her master, as tiny as the others, riding a newt.

Cherry pulled her head out of the water and took a breath. The whole garden seemed even more alive. There were Small People everywhere! Folk in the flowers, others leaping in the grasses, more swinging in the trees, plotting in the soil, catching birds as they landed in the bird bath and riding them as they flew across the garden! All of it was enchanted.

It was lucky that her master did not return until the evening because it took Cherry the whole day to compose herself. He rode up to the house on his horse, as tall as he had always been, and greeted Cherry warmly. His smile faltered for a moment, as he looked into her eye, but she directed him in for dinner and he thought no more of it.

After dinner he retreated to his chambers and Cherry heard voices and the sweetest music flowing up the dark corridor.

It grew louder and louder, until Cherry could bear it no more. She forced herself down that awful corridor and looked through the keyhole …

It was empty.

She could hear voices and music, but the room was totally empty except for the statues that circled the room and that coffin-shaped box.

She drew back, puzzled.

Then she tried looking with her other eye, the eye the ointment had gone on to. A vision appeared that couldn't have been more different. Inside she saw a whole host of ladies singing and dancing! Chandeliers hung from the ceiling and reflected candlelight on the glass floor.

It was not a coffin but a clavichord and the most beautiful woman lay upon it as her master filled the room with music. The woman's fingers curled through her master's hair and when he finished playing she leant down towards him and kissed him.

Cherry prickled with envy! She stormed back down the dark corridor and went to bed in tears and rage.

'Let's gather fruit today, Cherry, my dear,' said her master as she cleared away breakfast the following day.

Cherry helped as she always did, but she was distant, lost in silence. When he came to kiss her, she recoiled and held him back, 'I don't want to make anyone jealous,' she said in a resentful tone.

Anger flared dangerously in his eyes. 'You used the ointment, didn't you?' She had never seen him so angry. The sky darkened around them as an early night flooded above them. It started to rain.

He looked at her with sorrow in his eyes. 'You will leave immediately. Aunt Prudence will have to return. I will have no spy here.'

He brought out fine clothes he had prepared for Cherry, 'You must take these. These were to be yours.' She thought she detected grief in his words.

Wrapped in regret, she stored the bundle under one arm and held a lantern in her other hand, then she was instructed to follow him.

Under darkness of night, they left the garden. For miles and miles they walked through lanes and narrow passageways up a steep hill. As they came up on level ground it was just before daybreak.

'This is your last kiss, for you must be punished, but if you behave well I will return to the Lady Downs to see you.'

He disappeared as the sun rose and Cherry found herself back at the crossroads, the beautiful garden replaced by desolate moor.

Cherry didn't know how long she sat on that stone, but found the strength to pick herself up and return home.

Her parents thought they were seeing the ghost of their daughter as she drew up to the house. 'We thought you were dead.'

Cherry told her story, which everyone doubted, of course. But she never altered her tale, and so people grew to believe it. They say that Cherry was never quite the same afterwards, struck with grief or despair for what she had lost, or gained, during her time away.

Whenever the moon was full, she could be seen wandering on the Lady Downs dressed in the finest dress, waiting for that gentleman to return.

LOST CHILD OF ST ALLEN

St Allen, Cornwall

The origins of this changeling story go back to a document posthumously publishing the work of Mr Hals in 1750. Hals had recorded a story relating to a stolen child that took place in Trefronick a century before. The story has been embellished and changed through the subsequent centuries. It was used in 1922 by the Great Western Railway to draw holidaymakers to Cornwall.

It was a warm summer's evening in the hamlet of Trefronike in the parish of St Allen. The days were stretching as far as they can reach and the flowers of June were in full bloom.

It was not long 'til dinner time and the boy knew it, so he started picking flowers to take home to his mother, for the fields around the wood were a celebration of colour.

There were so many flowers to choose from, and although he didn't know their names, he knew he didn't have enough yet.

As he drew closer to the woods, he heard the most beautiful bird song and he stopped picking flowers to listen to it closer. The more he listened, the more he imagined it was something more than birds, for the sound of it had voices and instruments … Could it be that a band was playing in the wood so close to his house?

He followed the song into the woods and felt a glove of shadow touch his skin as he entered into the bosky shade. The music grew more and more compelling, melodious, exquisite, and elusive as a scent on the breeze.

He drew closer and closer to the dark centre of the wood but stopped by a thicket of knitted bramble and strings of clematis noose. The underwood was too thick to continue, and although the lure of the song pulled him toward it, he turned to go home.

He heard sounds of stretching vine and snapping rope, and turned around to see that invisible hands had pulled back the tangled plants, opening up a pathway just for him. He continued without difficulty, as if an invisible being were trampling down the foliage for easy passage.

Only a little further, the foliage gave way and the trees opened up to reveal a small lake. It was now the middle of the night, but it was hard to tell because the sky was a blaze of stars, shining brighter than he had ever known before.

The music raised to a grand crescendo and suddenly ceased.

Silence slipped over the lake as the boy fell into a deep sleep, nestled on a bed of fern.

When he opened his eyes again, the stars were surprisingly close. They moved backwards while they watched him regard them, and it was then that he realised they were Piskeys.

These Small People formed themselves into a procession, singing strange songs of words he did not know, in tunes he did not recognise.

One of the Small People beckoned the boy to join them. Together the procession journeyed into a hole in the earth, through to a strange land that the boy could only dream about for the rest of his life. They passed between pillars of crystal that held up arches of jewelled stone of every colour of the rainbow. The palaces of those folk far exceeded anything that was ever seen in the caverns of a Cornish mine.

His eyes filled with wonder, which seemed to delight the Small People who were so kind to him.

He did not remember much else, but he woke, sheltered in the fern he had fallen asleep in.

His parents had been beside themselves, of course, and when he was found, he was told a week had passed. They quizzed him as to how he had been spirited away and he told his tale. The eldest in the community said it must be a blessing indeed, for they who take children into their world do not always bring them back again. Perhaps his innocence and beauty had enchanted them? It was said that he had been carried through the waters to the Fairy abodes beneath them, and the old folk said that his would be a charmed life, and, so it was.

THE CHANGELING OF BREA VEAN

West Penwith, Cornwall

There are many changeling stories across the South West, but particularly across Cornwall. 'Betty Stogg's Baby' is a story similar to this one. Hunt (Popular Romances, 1865) included a version of the story as a poem 'The Spriggan's Child', which he notes 'was told by a Cornish Droll'. It is pretty horrific! A changeling is also seen in 'A Fairy Fair at Germoe', where the stolen baby is glimpsed in a Fairy fair.

It was believed there was a benevolent Piskey at the Mên-an-Tol stone formation who would change back a changeling if the babe was passed through the hole in the stone. Jenny Trayer found other ways to undo the spell.

'Lost Child of St Allen' was a particularly romanticised tale of a missing child. The reality would have been agonising with grief. I have chosen this version because I admire how Jenny continually faces adversity.

It was harvest time and the local people of furthest West Cornwall were called to help 'cut the neck'. They worked hard to get it done before the rain.

Jenny Trayer lived in Brea Vean at the foot of Carn Brea. Her babe was so young she didn't want to leave him, but she couldn't take him. She suckled him, rocked him to sleep in his cradle and spoke softly.

'I'll be away all day in the fields, my boy. Sleep deep and well and I'll be back before dark. I'll cross the fire hook and furze prong on the hearth for good luck. So, don't you worry my boy.' The baby was soon asleep and Jenny was out the door.

It took all day to cut the neck, and as soon as it was done and she was paid for her efforts she left the farm and headed home. The sky was darkening already, while behind her she heard her fellow workers celebrating 'cutting the neck'. But she had no time for that; she needed to get home.

The moon illuminated her journey like a warning and a guide. She opened the door and gasped to see a beam of moonlight flooding over the upturned cradle. Her baby was gone.

She scrabbled around the room, desperately calling for her child. Eventually she lit the wick of her iron lamp and saw a bit clearer.

She searched every dark spot, anywhere he could have crawled, but he was nowhere … he was missing. She calmed herself, trying not to panic. She told herself to breathe.

Once more, she went over the room, as carefully as she could. To her huge relief, in the wood corner, she found her boy nestled among the dried turf, ferns and furze. Relief and weariness hit her as she embraced the baby, letting it suckle. She was soon fast asleep.

Jenny woke up to the baby suckling. She was tired, so utterly drained. When she looked at him she had a strange feeling. He was hearty enough, but in the cool light of day there was something queer about him she couldn't place. He continually wanted food and never seemed satisfied. When she came to take him off her breast, he would roar like a bull. It was easier to let him drink, but it exhausted her. It was near impossible to get on with her chores … all winter it carried on like this. The neighbours shook their heads when they caught glimpses of mother and child.

'That child does nothing but eat, yet only wastes away,' they mumbled to each other. They all knew what must have happened to the boy, and Jenny knew it too.

She broke down finally, 'It's the Small People!'

An old neighbour said, 'Whether it is or not, you're doing the best you can, Jenny. But, mark my words, make sure you bathe the babe in the Chapel Uny Well as soon as May comes round.'

Winter was long and spring was slow coming. Jenny no longer saw her child when she looked at whatever *this* was … surely this ugly thing was a Spriggan? It looked at her with its terrible eyes and kept demanding more and more milk. May finally came, and on the first Wednesday Jenny wrapped the creature on her back and trudged over to Chapel Uny.

Desperate, she did not hesitate to dunk and drag it, widdershins, three times around the water of the well. There wasn't much change she could see after a week, so the next Wednesday she went back and did the same. The creature seemed to enjoy the ride and thrashed on her back with glee.

The next Wednesday was wet and wild; the Atlantic was in the sky that day, as Cornwall knows so well. But Jenny did not want to spoil the spell. She set off with the little brat on her shoulder while it screamed with joy and pulled at her hair. The wind blew around them in a wild rage and the thing seemed to enjoy it more than ever. It crowed like a cock in delight at the skies. Jenny held on to its foot in case it tried to escape. She prayed she would see her own babe again.

As they were rounding Chapel Uny Well, they were passing some rocks and a shrill voice called out, 'Tredrill! Tredrill! Thy wife and children greet thee well.'

Jenny stopped dead on the spot and looked everywhere for the voice. To her horror, the creature on her shoulder replied, shrill and loud …

For wife or child little care I!
They may laugh, or they may cry,
while milk I quaff, I stay so dry,
food for my fill, whenever I will,
on the dowdy's back ride,
with my legs astride,
When we work the spell
at the Chapel Well!

Jenny dropped the cursed thing to the ground; surely her heartstrings had snapped. She thought to abandon it, but she had no choice if she wanted to find her own son. She picked up the creature and ran the whole way home to Brea town. The creature was as wild as the wind, grabbing and screaming in its shrill voice. She couldn't take it and stopped not far from Brea Mansion. She pulled the clinging creature off her and threw it down into a dung heap.

She burst into tears. A group of women hurried out of the farm to see what the matter was. Jenny shook as she recalled to them what she had just heard the changeling say to the invisible voice.

Their faces all turned deadly serious. 'Didn't I tell thee, months ago, that thee had a changeling there, Jenny? Ever since that neck-cuttin night, thy own child was spirited away and that thing left in his place.'

The women watched as the creature squirmed in the mud, squinting at them. One of the women dropped her voice and brought Jenny into a close circle.

'I know what you need to do … Under night's cover, build a fire of dried green fern. Get the house as smoky as possible. When the smoke is so thick you can no longer bear it, leave the changeling on the hearth stone, get out of the house, turn three times, then you can enter back into the house and your baby will be back.'

'No,' said the eldest there. 'That's superstition. Have you ever seen it work?' The woman shook her head. 'Lucky for ee I can tell ee how you can get rid of this Bucca for good, and save your own dear cheeld. Ashes. You'll need to lay the creature in the ashes of fire and beat it with a broom. Then, under cover of darkness, lay it naked on a church stile. Keep out of sight, mind, n' make sure you can't hear nothing. Nine times out of ten this works, tried and tested.'

A bucket of ashes and a broom was near at hand, so they turned the bucket out and placed the changeling in the midst of it and beat the child there and then. The changeling made such a terrible noise, all of them were certain it was working.

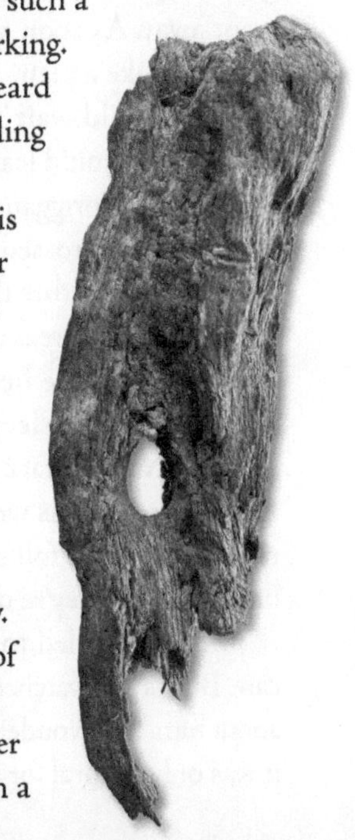

Dame Ellis, who lived at Brea Mansion, heard the commotion and came running out demanding to know what on earth was going on.

Jenny says, 'Why mistress. That thing there is not my cheeld, but a changeling in 'tis place. Ever since I was reapan in your field that day we cut the neck. My child was spirited away and this … this thing. Has given me no end of trouble since. The neighbours all know it. It's been nonstop screechan, suckan, eatan and refused to grow or use its legs.'

Dame Ellis was appalled at them all.

'But that's nothing,' pressed Jenny urgently. She told her of the shrill voice that came out of the creature by the well.

Dame Ellis looked stern and pointed a finger at Jenny. 'I believe thou wert either drunk or in a waking dream, girl. Which was it? Shame on you! Harm this infant no more. Take it home and wash it well, feed it regular and never leave it laying all day in its cradle again. Call for the doctor if you cannot care for the child yourself.'

Dame Ellis walked back inside. The women waited in silence until the door was closed.

'She is an unbeliever, she has more money than care,' they said to reassure Jenny. 'Besides, she couldn't tell a Spriggan from a Knocker, or a Piskey.'

Jenny knew it was the truth, but the dame's husband was Squire Ellis, landlord to each one of them. He would be well aware of his wife's thoughts on this matter. They would need to be careful.

The women hurried home with Jenny, the creature back on her back. They did nothing rash. They made dinner and spoke like nothing was amiss.

Squire Ellis silently slipped down to Jenny's house, waited at her door and listened to the voices talking inside. He stayed there for a good long while and, deciding there was nothing untoward going on, went away. As soon as they heard him go, they knew the coast was clear to make a plan.

They would wait 'til the lights had gone out in the great house before they would leave the cottage. Jenny and another woman took the bantling Spriggan up Brea town and on to the stile on the churchway path that crossed a field on Brea Lane. Under the cloak of night, they left the creature that had been such a nuisance naked on the stile.

The day was breaking when Jenny returned to the stile. She hoped and prayed to see her own child, and sure enough she found her own babe softly sleeping. He was sparkling clean, the rosy glow shining from his face again. 'My cheeld! Oh my cheeld!' said Jenny. She noticed he was wrapped in a piece of gay flowery chintz, the type that those small folks are known to covet and steal from the furze bushes when they're drying in the sun.

She was thrilled to have her boy back and nursed him with great care. But as she watched him grow, she knew there was something queer about him. She wondered if he was still in the Fairies' power, but decided it was only natural for someone who had been under their influence.

He was a sensitive soul, and when he had only just learned to walk he would wander off to all sorts of out-of-the-way places. Jenny had a job of keeping an eye on him. He always seemed half in this world, half in another. He spoke to himself a lot too, whenever he played, or whenever he was walking in the green lanes. The community were convinced it was the Little People he spoke to.

Dame Ellis often came to visit the boy and brought him many nice things that Jenny could never afford. Jenny appreciated the kindness of the good lady of Brea, even if the Dame did give the most disapproving looks when anyone referred to him as 'the Changeling'.

At the age of 9, the squire took the boy into employment to tend to the animals, which he was excellent at. He had a way with creatures. But he had to be monitored at work because he had a tendency to wander off, sometimes for days on end. But, in lambing season there was no one better to have around. No lamb was ever lost when he was present.

He was never at full health. He had strange fits now and again, and his mother looked after him when these got really bad. Still, he grew up to be a well-liked young man.

It was not entirely unusual then when one day he went missing. After three days, his flock were tracked down and he was found, sleeping in the rushes. His face was a smile as if he was in the happiest dream, but the poor changeling of Brea was dead.

TREVILLEY CLIFFS

West Penwith, Cornwall

William Bottrell recorded the tale of 'Trevilley Cliffs' as a footnote after 'The Faerie Dwelling at Selena Moor' in his 1873 Traditions and Hearthside Stories of West Cornwall.

Both stories beguile and enchant me, and I believe the tale of 'Trevilley Cliffs' is worth much more than a footnote. It stands alone in its enchantment and takes place among one of the most spectacular landscapes in Britain, so I include it here first.

Trevilley cliffs stand between Nanjizal beach and Land's End. The granite extrusions have become softened by relentless weather, which, in radiant summer sunshine, makes them look like gentle giants. This bay is where the Michael and Mary ley line is believed to begin its journey across southern England's ancient and sacred sites.

I met farmer and sculptor Aidan Hicks, whose family has farmed the land reaching up to Trevilley cliffs for generations. He is an avid runner and runs along the cliff paths. He told me that there is a certain part of Trevilley cliffs that makes him speed up because he feels uncomfortable. When he told me his grandmother's maiden name was Vingoe I had to tell him this story …

Somewhere along Trevilley cliffs, Richard Vingoe had lost his way. How on earth he had managed it, he did not know. His father farmed this land and he had grown up exploring it all. He thought he knew it like the back of his hand. But he was baffled. His father would be ashamed when he found out.

He found a pathway that led down to the water's edge. He just needed to see the horizon and he would be able to reorient himself. The tight path took him through narrow rock walls that glowed green with bubbling seaweed. He entered into an underground passage, something like a cavern. A glowing light pulled him forward and he emerged into a pleasant-looking place, green with meadows and bounty-filled trees.

This was definitely not his farm! How was this possible? It was all utterly new to him; the air was almost green.

Walking on, he was relieved to hear sounds of merry making. He drew towards voices and discovered a place where people were playing games.

He noticed a number of people hurling, and as he approached them the silver ball flew towards him. He was fond of the game, and keen to introduce himself to find out where he was. He stepped forward to pick up the ball, when an alarmed voice behind him called out, 'Don't!'

A beautiful lady was hiding behind a large boulder. She made signs for him to leave the ball and beckoned him towards her. She led him into an orchard grove, where she turned to face him.

She seemed familiar, but he couldn't quite place her.

A wave of realisation dawned on him, 'But, I know you. Aren't you … Didn't you … die, a few years ago?'

'Not dead! I have been changed into a Fairy state because I trespassed here and joined in their game … I picked up their ball. There is no way back if you pick up the ball!' A shadow of sadness passed over her face. 'You are on the edges of the Otherlands. Do not take another step. I am bound to endlessly serve these Small People, but there is time to save you.'

'Please, remind me of your name?'

'Don't you remember me, my love?'

He looked at her deeply, his eyes unclouded and grief hit him.

'But, we were to be married! We were in love! We buried you. How is this possible?'

'Follow me,' she directed him away.

She led him up a hidden path away from the hurlers and the spectators of the game, and they crawled their way into darkness, through a rocky cavern until they saw the light of the upper world. It was a much shorter road than the one he had entered.

He paused, 'Won't you come with me? I don't want to lose you again.'

'There is no chance to save me now. Besides, you have life ahead of you … You must go! Richard, I know you are to be married, and it pleases me that you have found happiness. You must go,' she said.

Richard felt his heart break all over again. Suddenly he wanted to call the wedding off, knowing that his first love was alive after all this time! 'How can I go on, knowing you are here?'

'If you really must know your mind, hold your engagement for three years. That shall reveal your heart. Now go!'

Richard Vingoe crawled out of a cairn on the cliff, overlooking Ninjizel. He turned back to look for his love, but she had vanished.

'I will wait three years.'

He was found sleeping on that cairn, a week after he had gone missing. After the strange event, he seemed forever changed.

His engagement was called off. The story suggests he never found his way back to that pleasant country. Bottrell tells us that he took hard to drink and died unmarried.

THE FAIRY DWELLING AT SELENA MOOR

West Penwith, Cornwall

This is one of the most outstanding tales from Pixieland. I recommend reading Bottrell's original – it is richly told with detail. When I first came across it, I assumed Bottrell was a true Victorian romantic, adding every bit of detail he could. However, I think the truth is that he knew this location extraordinarily well, and he knew the farms and the people, and he grew up hearing these stories, so it's possible he poured all of himself into his telling.

Jeremy Harte, in his brilliant book Explore Fairy Traditions, *postulates that this could be an Irish story that has relocated to Cornwall. A 'sham' body is more common in Irish mythology, while it doesn't appear in Cornish changeling folklore anywhere else.*

Bottrell presents two versions of the story (this and 'Trevilley Cliffs') geographically close to each other, suggesting the story has been in place for a time.

When the ancient family of Noy flourished in St Buryan there was a large tract of unenclosed common belonging to the farms of Pendrea, Selena and Tresidder. A great part of this land was inaccessible swamp where a labyrinth of water pathways streamed through the quaking bog. It was alive with life. Starry white flowers of the bogbean grew alongside the pink cuckoo flowers and nodding heads of cotton grass.

Down a one-way track along the edge of this wetland lived Mr Noy. He rode his horse along the dense thicket of elder and blackthorn, which knitted together like castles among gorse and brambles. It was a spectacle throughout the year. In summer the skylark would break into song, as if she was calling out to him. Even in winter it was frequented by visiting wildfowl.

It was late September and Mr Noy and many other helpers had been called to the neighbouring farm of Burnewhall to help the Pendars. It was harvest time and the next day was to be the harvest festival of Gulthise (harvest home). It was a great celebration, marking the final day of bringing in the corn. A grand feast was being prepared to be shared with all who had helped, and it was the custom to invite the elders in the poor house to join the festivities, too.

More hands were needed if they were to be finished by the next evening, so Mr Noy was asked to ride over to St Buryan to find help.

'Make sure you ask the sexton,' requested Dame Pendar. 'See if he will bring his fiddle … maybe he will enchant us with a story, he is such an enchanting droll teller.'

Mr Noy met up with the sexton, the parson and the clerk in the Ship Inn and a good group of them agreed to come and help the following day.

The new recruits turned up to help in the fields, but there was no sign of Mr Noy. After a long day, the harvest was finally brought in and he had still not been seen. Tankards of cider and ale clattered together in cheer as the Gulthise feasting began. And what a feast it was! Roast and boiled beef, mutton, squab pies, rabbit and puddings galore were shared, but Dame Pendar couldn't rid herself of a feeling of unease. Where was Mr Noy?

There was much music, merriment and drinking, and the sexton shared many stories. Quietly, Dame Pendar sent off messengers to go and check in with the neighbouring farms to enquire whether Mr Noy had been held up helping others.

The dancing and singing kept them all up late, and the messengers returned just as the feast was breaking up. No one had seen him, and worse, his horse and his dogs hadn't returned home after visiting the Ship Inn. Concern spilt out over the good cheer.

'He must have enjoyed himself too hard at the Ship Inn,' someone said to ease the building atmosphere. But others knew that wasn't like him. Anxiety grew as the sun rose that day and search parties went out to all the places they could think that he might be.

After a day of searching, there was still no joy. Dame Pendar's imagination grew dark. The mill ponds and streams and cliffs and all other dangerous places were checked, but no trace of Mr Noy. Neither his horse nor his dogs could be found.

The whole community came out in force to help search further and further afield, but to the horror of all it was as if he had vanished entirely.

On the third day, a party went to double-check if any news had arrived at Mr Noy's house. He lived alone, for even though he was late into his thirties he remained a bachelor.

As they were riding along the track that ran beside the marsh along the Pendrea side of Selena Moor, a whining dog was heard through the thickets and the pools of the impenetrable wetland. The dogs started barking as soon as they heard people and the search party got off their horses and made their way toward them. On a little island in the bog were Mr Noy's two dogs and on another grassy bank, his horse whinnied with delight to see people. The dogs were half starved, but would not leave the place. They pointed their noses towards the thick furze and brambles that must have grown there for hundreds of years.

The search party battled their way through, dodging the quaking bog between tuft and island, squeezing between the scratching foliage. Deeper and deeper they went and were amazed to discover an old ruin in the thick of it all, surrounded by old skaw (elder) trees dripping heavily in deep purple berries.

No one had any idea that there was a ruin here, and by the look of it, it had been lost to time for eons. It was cloaked in moss, crowned with ferns and choked by brambles. The dogs barked incessantly. They pushed through until they could see the body of Mr Noy lying on the ground, seemingly asleep.

It was difficult to rouse him, but, at last he woke and rubbed his eyes.

'But, I know you!' he exclaimed. 'You're Pendrea folk. How have you come here? I have journeyed so far from home. What parish is this? Did my dogs go all the way home to find you?'

He seemed dazed and confused and as stiff as a board as they helped him up. They gave him some brandy, and with no small effort got him back to his horse. They found the best pathway through the bog, and even though he was told he was only half a mile from his home, he refused to believe he wasn't in a faraway land.

They crossed the running water that divided the farms and suddenly the enchantment broke. With amazement, Mr Noy recognised where he was.

'How extraordinary! I'm so glad we'll be back in time for the Gulthise,' he said with returning cheer.

When they told him that the corn had been carried in three days before, he said they must be joking, and he refused to believe it until he saw it all roped down under the thatch barn. He touched them all to make sure it was no dream.

'But, I haven't been away long enough.'

The word spread fast that Mr Noy had been found. The tension that held the farm broke like dawn. He sat by a blazing fire and was brought a bowl of breakfast as Dame Pendar and a crowd of neighbours gathered to hear his tale.

'I left the ship and it was such a clear night, I felt I could see every star in the sky, so I thought I might shave the last mile off my journey by taking a short cut across the moor.

'It was an animal path really, but I had seen it once or twice in the summer, and it really was such a clear evening so I chanced it. My horse wanted to keep to the usual road,' he said, 'but I pulled her back towards the moor, so that we took the path unknown.'

Everything began to look alarmingly unnatural, so he decided to turn back and retrace his steps, but the way back could not be found.

They went on like that for miles and miles, and all the time his dogs were whining. Finally, his horse stubbornly refused to go on. 'I tried to pull the horse, but there was no chance.'

A look of dazed confusion cast a shadow over his face then. 'I went on to discover a path, but it felt like I travelled for miles and miles more, and I couldn't understand how I had become so lost. It really is only a small bit of marsh to my house. To my relief, I heard music and followed it till I spied lights glimmering through the trees.'

The festivities gave him hope, for of course it seemed to him that he had arrived at a farm where a Gulthise was in full swing.

People were moving behind and between the trees, and he made his way through an orchard into a meadow. He saw hundreds of people, seated at tables, eating and drinking with great enjoyment, while others danced to a band that played. The dancers moved so fast, he could not count them, and when he tried his head became giddy with the continual whirling. He felt caught in a river, pulled this way and that, until he saw a damsel in a white dress playing a tambourine by the house.

His eyes caught on her and it was then he realised all the other revellers were so much smaller than she was. He had not noticed before.

Mr Noy said he looked back at the damsel in white and found her reassuring, as if she were a tidal node amongst a swelling ocean. He could not take his eyes away from her. In a brief moment when one dance ended and before the next began, it occurred to him that she looked familiar.

The woman in white spotted him too, and she gave her tambourine to another fellow. The woman made her way towards him, topping up tankards for those Small Folk as she walked past their tables. The folk cheered and a new song began, calling new dancers to the floor.

'The music was so charming,' he said to his audience. 'It took all my willpower not to join in with gay abandon. But the woman had a frown so sharp it pointed at me, and it helped me resist the urge to dance.'

She begged him to follow her, around the corner of the house, out of sight. She led him into a clear spot, where, under the moonlight, he suddenly recognised her. His heart stopped …

'As I live and breathe, it was Grace Hutchens, my sweetheart,' Mr Noy said to the stunned crowd. They all knew her: the daughter of the farmer at Selena. She had died three or four years ago; at least they had all mourned her as dead. He had thrown soil on her coffin as it lowered into Buryan Churchyard.

'I put my hands out to hold her,' Mr Noy continued ...

> 'Get back!' Grace cried, 'Do not touch me. It is not safe, my dear love. Touch nothing here. No fruit, nor flower. For eating a plum in this enchanted orchard was my undoing. Thank the stars my dear William that I was able to stop you. My heart could not bear it if you were trapped in this place too.'
>
> 'But I … *we*, thought you were dead. How can this be?'
>
> 'It was a sham body you found dead on the moor. What was buried in my place was nothing but a changeling. My body is very much here.'
>
> 'How?'
>
> 'I wanted to surprise you at your home, William. I crossed the moor, I knew it was only a little way, but I grew lost … I found this place and I was so very hungry, so I ate a plum and …'
>
> Several little voices squeaked, 'Grace, Grace, bring us more cider.'
>
> Grace's eyes became serious, 'Remain behind the house at all times. Do not touch a flower or a fruit, or your life will be forfeit.'
>
> 'But, I would love a sip of cider,' he said with a chancing smile.
>
> 'No, my love, I'm serious, don't touch a thing. It would mean death. Await me here, I'll soon return.' Tears sparkled like stars in her eyes as she turned and hurried off.
>
> She was back in a few moments and led William deeper down a shaded path, where the music and merriment didn't overpower their voices. 'You know, my dear Will, that I love you so much, you can never know how much. How I wish our future had not been stolen from us.'

She couldn't say how long she had been in this place. After she ate the plum, something hollowed inside her, something terrible detached her from life. When she woke she found herself surrounded by hundreds of Small People, who were thrilled that she was there with them.

'We have been wanting a tidy girl who would keep our home decent and nurse the children.' They spoke with glee, and then sadness, 'We are not so strongly made as we used to be.'

'They have children?'

'Very few,' she said sadly. 'Only two have been born since I have been here and they have such grand celebrations to honour their arrivals. And every little man, however old, is proud to be called the father.'

'But they can't all be the father,' said Mr Noy incredulously.

'You must remember, they are not of our religion. They are star worshippers and are forever changing their mind or their partner by whim or fancy. I should think constancy would be quite tiresome for them.

'The eldest of them wither away until one can almost see through them, like puffs of smoke. These seem vainer than any other, though I know they long for the time when they are set free from the weariness of having no hope or intention ...'

'My darling Grace. This is no place for you to be. Let us escape, otherwise I will stay here with you.'

She looked at William and so wanted to touch him.

'Would it be so bad if I joined you?' he said.

'It is a world of illusion, William. A total sham. They have no hearts, and such little sense of the richness of feeling. I believe they were mortals once, however many hundreds or thousands of years ago it might've been.'

'But what sustains you?' Mr Noy asked.

'Honey-dew and berries are all any of us eat. Oh what I would do for a bit of salted fish. But the goat milk is something I relish.'

He looked at her quizzically. 'Goat milk?'

'Goats are lured through cairns and other out-of-the-way places. Piskeys, disguised as he-goats, are sent out as decoys to find the best milkers. We all relish the milk, but they especially nourish the babies and changelings.'

Looking at Mr Noy with a melancholic expression, she sighed and continued, 'I am getting used to this sort of life. It isn't quite as bad as it might be. I am at their service at all times, but the whole tribe treat me with great kindness. They love me … in their way.'

Mr Noy felt dizzy all of a sudden, and it must have shown on his face. 'Oh my dear, sweet William. Don't be jealous. They are nothing but vapour, and feeling is no more substantial than capricious fancy.'

'I want to stay here,' he pleaded.

'We have talked too long, really, William, you must go. But, if it brings you comfort, know this. I am able to take the form of a bird. Over these past years I have visited you when you have been grieving me. I shall continue to do so. When you are old and tired of life, perhaps then return here and we can dwell together in this Fairyland of the moors. As long as life fills your lungs, let nature preserve you.'

Shrill voices sounded from the Small Folk. 'Grace! Grace! Where art thou so long?'

Grace got up to return to them.

Suddenly Mr Noy had an idea. He knew the Small Folk couldn't abide a garment turned inside out, and they were likely to flee if they saw one. Feeling his glove in his pocket, he took it out and, quicker than a thought, turned it inside out. He dropped a stone into it and threw it among the crowd.

In an instant the Small Folk, Grace, the building, music, everything, vanished ...

'The house became a roofless ruin and suddenly all became thickets. The brambles rambled around me like wild creatures, and something hit me over my head and that's all I remember.'

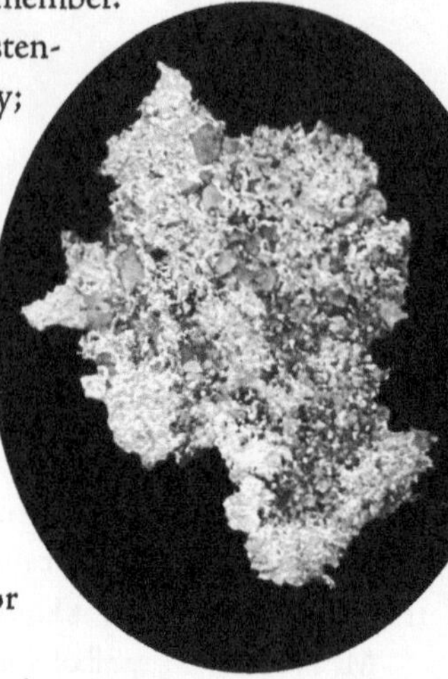

The hush that had fallen over his listeners back at the farm was extraordinary; even the fire was silent. He felt the crowd's attention upon him, almost as if it were visible.

He looked at their faces, and realised that some of those Small Folk bore resemblance to the people of his community looking back at him now. Had he seen some of their relatives, stolen away to be changelings in that strange place, or ancestors lost long ago?

William Noy was said to be a changed man after he had strayed into the Small People's habitation. He could barely talk of anything other than what he had seen and heard that evening. Every time a robin or a wagtail or any other familiar bird was seen or heard, he wondered if it might be his dearly departed love.

Often at dusk on moonless nights he would set out looking for Grace. Over the coming year, he became melancholy, neglected his farm and grew tired of company. Before the next harvest, the body of dear Mr Noy was found on the marsh.

Whether he died or it was a sham body, left as he went to find Grace, no one ever knew.

8

BY PIXIE FEET: THE HILLS *ARE* ALIVE!

Cornwall is alive with raw Atlantic energy, impossibly beautiful scenery and rare light. No wonder the Cornish culture is so rich in language and identity. It is a landscape that has inspired imaginations of artists for centuries: Barbara Hepworth, John Wells, Wilhelmina Barns-Graham and Ithell Colquhoun, among many others, who have made visceral work responding to the influence of the landscape.

It has been postulated that the vast amount of stories, legends and folklore of spirits of the land recorded in West Penwith may contain remnants of pre-christian belief systems. How far back do these memories go? These questions remain a glorious mystery, but the fact that the stories and traditions have been recorded, speaks to the proud identity and culture that remains in Cornwall today.

Where you find people, you find stories, and where there are stories, beliefs are shaped. I find it interesting that the further east we travel, the more stories there are linking the Pixies and the Church. There is bound to be tension between the Church and anything that resembles a supposed antithesis of an ideology. Perhaps this is no surprise as these stories were recorded in a time when religion would have significantly dominated the social and cultural landscape.

No time to wait, there is still much exploring to do. There are places we have not been.

ORIGIN OF THE PIXIES

Somerset

Home of much British magic, Somerset boasts a stunning array of landscapes, with its internationally important wetlands, broad-leaved woodlands, grass and heathlands. Whether you're in the Mendips or the Levels, you will be close to a story hidden in the landscape.

The marshy wetlands around Glastonbury are said to hold the ancient doorways to Avalon and the Faerie realms.

In 1191 Glastonbury Abbey claimed to hold the final resting places of Britain's most loved king, Arthur, and his Guinevere. If you speak to locals, however, they may disagree. I can tell you that Arthur and his knights sleep under Cadbury Hill, ready and waiting for Britain's greatest peril. In our most desperate hour of need, Arthur will return, defend the land he loves and take his position as the once and future king.

Glastonbury town continues to draw earth lovers to its white and red springs. I was taken to the white spring by storytellers Sharon Jacksies and Jem Dick on a wonderful weekend, exploring Somerset and its living stories. Before the building that currently houses the white spring was built, it is said the sacred waters issued forth from a now-destroyed crystal cave. This place is one of the ancient doors into the Faerie realm.

I am indebted to the marvellous storyteller Sharon Jacksties for the following tale. She is a particular expert on Somerset stories and when she tells them, the landscape is brought into radiant life.

Back in the distant days, after the fall of Heaven, Lucifer made his new home deep in darkness and amassed spirits to do his bidding.

Many of them complied to his will, but he found others tricksy and unmanageable. He called them his Imps, but they were not really *his*, they were just creatures that thrived in the dark solitary places and refused to leave.

Lucifer locked them up in an eternal labyrinth he called Hell. He watched them, determined that he would eventually bend them to his will and put them to his dark deeds. He watched as they gnawed on the metal bars of Hell. They particularly liked playing with locks, and could adapt and manipulate metal with remarkable skill. Every time Lucifer returned from leading mortals into temptation, he would find that the Imps had made new mischief. Either they had undone the locks, or created ingenious traps within traps that Lucifer himself would have had a hard time solving.

Tricksy indeed they were. From then on, Lucifer decided that whenever he had business to attend to, he would leave a guard to keep watch on his Imps.

One day, Lucifer left a mortal soul to watch over the Imps. In life, the man had been called Jan, and he looked like he didn't have much imagination or wit, so Lucifer thought him subservient enough.

Alone and oppressed, Jan felt the fear of darkness. He had not been a bad man when he was alive – his mother had yearned for him to read the Bible and to go to church, but he had not really been into any of it. She asked him to always carry a copy of the Bible with him, so that he need never feel alone.

He had been true to her on that request. It was a very useful object. He had lived in Somerset, and so many of their tavern tables had wobbly legs. He would slide the copy of his Bible under the uneven leg and he never spilt a sip of beer. Out in the fields the Bible would come out at lunchtime too; it was a perfect surface to eat his lunch of cheese and bread off.

He sat in Hell, looking towards the bars that bound those dangerous creatures in the darkness. Their murky eyes flashed at him and he felt so very afraid.

He hugged himself and realised the Bible was still in his pocket. His mother's words rang out in his mind and, like a miracle, even on the edges of Hell he didn't feel so alone. His grin even creased up a bit … how had he managed to sneak a Bible into Hell? The cheese-encrusted cover did hide the words 'Holy Bible'.

Jan opened the book and did something he had never done before. He started reading the words. It was a book of stories and they were all new to him. He read them out loud, slow and sober, and, amazingly, they gave him some cheer.

Rich imagery of humans and hope, landscapes and miracles flooded into his words, and stories illuminated the depths of darkness.

The Imps were fascinated by the words dancing into life. They broke free from the bars that held them, and stepped into the dim light where Jan sat. They sat in a circle around the reader and listened with curiosity.

They were ugly and unusual, but they were not so frightening after all. He could see they were curious – they had fire in their eyes. He continued reading, this time with more intent … He now had an audience. More Imps came, hundreds of them, thousands. They unlocked the deepest depths of the prisons of darkness in order to hear the stories being shared.

Lucifer happened to be in Somerset at that time, suggesting sin and splashing slippery despair into lovers' dreams, when he felt it.

The depths of his stomach turned, wild with unease. He returned in a flash of lightning.

'What in Hell's name is going on?' he screamed and gasped with horror as he looked at his Imps. They all had light in their eyes. They were ruined! 'What have you done to my Imps?' he wailed over and over again.

Lucifer could not believe that this halfwit human had smuggled such dangerous contraband into Hell. Jan was banished to walk indefinitely on earth for his terrible deeds. It is said that he wanders Somerset still, sharing cheese, propping up tables with an old book, and sometimes he tells tall tales, too.

Some tell it was Jan who picked up a lantern and became known as Jack O'Lantern.

Every last Imp was turned out of Hell, but they left their traps unlocked so there is always a way out.

They found refuge on the earth's surface somewhere around Somerset. They found the most wonderful dark places cloaked in moss, under bosky shade, deep in rock, near the throaty laughter of rivers.

Lucifer cursed them to be burnt by iron in punishment. But they remained curious to the nature of metal. Many explored deep into the seams of ore, eternally knocking down in the mines. Others were endlessly fascinated by gold, or with silver coins.

The spirits covered the earth, but mostly kept to themselves. Still, they have not forgotten the power of story and brush up against the humans from time to time, to listen in to tales being told.

Wherever they made their home in the South West, their human neighbours called them the Piskeys, Pisgies or Pixies.

THE PISKIES

by Sir Arthur Quiller-Couch

We were not good enough for Heaven,
Not bad enough for Hell:
And therefore unto us 'twas given
Unseen on earth to dwell:

To listen by the moonlit thatch,
By window-blinds to lurk,
To watch men on their knees, and watch
Men go about their work.

We watch in hope to be forgiven;
But still we cannot tell
Whose deeds are good enough for Heaven,
Whose bad enough for Hell.

PIXIE QUARTET

Dartmoor, Devon

There was a wonderful account on the Modern Fairy Sighting podcast of a lady who went for a walk in the woods near Berry Pomeroy, Devon. She sat down on a log and something moved in her peripheral vision.

She looked around to see a small creature skipping up towards her, at which point it slapped her across her face and ran away laughing.

One day a shepherd boy fell asleep in the midst of his flock not realising that a quartet of Pixies were close by. They thought it would be wildly funny to play a little game. The first Pixie jumped over the old stone wall and fastened the boy to the ground, locking his eyes shut. The second Pixie tickled his nose with a beard of barley. The third ran around the field screaming 'Wolf! Wolf!' at the poor sheep, while the fourth bewitched a beguiling charm on each of the animals. Soon every sheep had leapt over the walls in all directions and they were wonderfully Pixy-led.

How the Pixies laughed and laughed at the boy, frozen in helpless agony, but they released him soon enough. The poor lad got up and ran into the nearest gorse bush, covering himself in scratches and bruises.

Job well done, thought the Pixies, who released the charm on the lost sheep and led them all back home again.

OTTERY BELLS

Ottery St Mary, Devon

There is a mixed reaction to bells from the Pixies. As we have seen in 'Withypool Dingdogs', the Pixies did not like the noisy disturbance of church bells. But as we have also seen, in 'Fairy Funeral', the Piskeys chose to bury their queen in a church ringing a sorrow-filled bell. To confuse the issue further, Anna Bray wrote the story 'Church Rock' in Peep at the Pixies *(1853), inspired by the folk belief that every Sunday the sounds of church bells would peal out through an enchanted rock near Merrivale on Dartmoor. Bray writes that the rock was destroyed by a farmer, who received great wrath from the angry Pixies.*

In flower lore there are many bell-shaped flowers that are associated with the Fae folk; wood sorrel is called 'fairy-bell' in Wales. Bluebells, heather bells and harebells are all potential Fairy hats, or musical instruments with which to dance the night away.

The ultimate church bell story is from East Devon.

The Bishop of Exeter was travelling through East Devon and came to the settlement of Otteri (known today as Ottery St Mary). He was enchanted by the 'untouched' spot, where the gentle River Otter flowed through green meadows and past woods on its way to the sea. The place was so full of beauty that he was moved to celebrate it.

'This is the perfect spot to build a church. For the sound of church bells to be heard.'

Without hesitation, he began organising it. He commissioned architects, builders and labourers, and, of course, a set of bells were ordered from a foundry in Wales.

The place was indeed enchanted, and along the sandstone riverbank there was much cause for concern.

The Pixies' long ears had heard the intentions of this meddling minister.

'Ding Dongs?'

'I don't think so!'

'Noisy clattering, sky shattering, church bells?'

'I think not.'

So, the Pixies got to work.

In Wales, the bells were being made, but as each bell was cast, mysterious droplets of dew appeared just at the wrong moment and made the castings crack. Bell after bell was ruined.

Mystified, the workers remade them until eventually a full set was complete.

The foundry had kept in touch with the bishop, and he suspected some sort of magical trickery might be afoot. Concerned for their journey to Devon, the bishop organised an escort of monks to chaperone the bells to Otteri. The Pixies could feel the weight of impending doom travelling towards them.

They danced a spell around the monks *and* those dreaded bells, so that they lost their way and journeyed right past Otteri towards the cliffs at Sidmouth.

The monks never would have noticed a thing and would have all fallen to their deaths, but, inches away from the cliff's edge, a monk stubbed his toe and uttered the words 'Oh bless my soul', which broke the Pixy-leading enchantment. The monks made their way safely to Otteri and the bells were installed in the two church towers.

But the mischief was not yet over.

The Pixies darted up to the towers, and faster than a moonbeam wove gossamer threads around the clapper of every bell.

There were special prayers in the church below for the bells and great commotion in excitement to hear the first sound of them. The ringers pulled the ropes, but no sound came from the tower.

The Pixies were thrilled; their homes were safe.

But that pesky bishop sent someone up to check on the bells and he cut through the gossamer thread, whereupon they finally rang out.

But the Pixies had not finished.

Under cover of dusk one midsummer's morning in June 1454, the Pixies returned. They waited near the church for the bell-ringers to arrive. One by one, they spirited away Otteri's ringers and imprisoned them all in a secret location along the river valley.

About a mile away from the town, along the River Otter, a group of confused bell-ringers found themselves stuck in a sandstone hollow with a ceiling formed by old tree roots. The Pixies were jubilant. Their plan had finally worked.

Without any bell-ringers to pull those dratted ropes, there would be no terrible noises.

However, their celebrations did not last. Disaster and devastation tore the sky in two as the bells of Otteri rang out that midsummer morn. The Pixies realised they could not stop the tide. In misery, the Pixies abandoned their home and sought refuge where peace could be found.

The vicar is said to have found the bellringers, who told their story and revealed the cave to the people of Otteri. Ever since that day the underground hollow has become known as the Pixies' Parlour.

This folk tale is brought to life every year on Pixie Day in Ottery St Mary. The Saturday closest to the midsummer solstice is celebrated by hundreds of Brownies, Beavers, Cubs, Rainbows, Guides and Scouts groups, who dress as Pixies and flood into the town's park to act out the 'Pixies' Revenge'.

The Pixies kidnap the bell-ringers and bring them into the park, where a bell-ringer eventually escapes.

I was totally charmed when I visited in 2024. It is a quintessentially bonkers and charming English fete, and has real Pixie spirit. The town's green space is filled with entertainers, who build up the anticipation for the grand climax of the day, the re-enactment of the 'Pixies' Revenge'. Ottery is also famous for its tar barrel evening on 5 November. Both of these events have an incredibly mischievous, wild energy and honour not only the people of Ottery and their ancestors, but the spirit of the place, too.

Generations of adventure seekers have sought out the Pixies' Parlour, and many initials and Pixie images have been carved into the walls by those who have found it. Among the names and initials carved into the wall is that of Samuel Taylor Coleridge, who was born in Ottery.

In the summer of 1793, aged 21, he chaperoned a party of young ladies to the Pixies' Parlour and proclaimed one as the Faery Queen. He subsequently wrote 'Song of the Pixies' inspired by the event, which was one of the first times the Pixies were brought to a literary audience.

> Whom the untaught Shepherds call
> Pixies in their madrigal,
> Fancy's children, here we dwell:
> Welcome, Ladies! to our cell
>
> *Songs of the Pixies*, Samuel Taylor Coleridge, 1793

ST NONNA'S WELL

Peylant, Cornwall

Also known as St Nun's Well/St Ninnie's Well/Piskies Well.

Grandson of Jonathan Couch, Sir Arthur Quiller-Couch was a prolific writer and literary critic who published under the pseudonym Q. Kenneth Grahame was a friend and stayed with Quiller-Couch at Fowey while he was writing The Wind in the Willows. *It is said that the character Ratty is based on Quiller-Couch (Guardian, 2010).*

In his Ancient and Holy Wells of Cornwall *(1894), Quiller-Couch records his experience of uncovering and tending to St Nonna's Well at Peylant. Quiller-Couch was taken to the well by a woman, who told him that she had used it for divination purposes in her younger days. It had been smothered by time and weather, and lay hidden beneath dense undergrowth of willow and bramble. The well's stone chamber had become dislodged by an old oak tree. He organised the clearing and restoration, felling the oak and rebuilding the structure that housed the well.*

Quiller-Couch recorded that 'the inside of the well is draped with the luxury and fronds of hart's-tongue and black spleenwort ferns, on a rich bed of moss and liverwort. At the farther end of the floor is a round granite basin with a deeply moulded brim, ornamented lower and all round its circumference with a series of rings, each enclosing a Greek cross or ball' (Quiller-Couch, 1894, p.175).

The well was believed to be the haunt of a 'beneficial elf' who offered health and good fortune to the reverent. Offerings of coins and bent pins would be left at the well to appease the spirit, but the elf would show enduring anger to any who desecrated it. Quiller-Couch remarks that a great number of pins were found in the basin during its restoration.

Alex Langstone notes that during the 1960s the Rev. A. Lane-Davies recorded the horror a lady felt when she discovered her children had brought home eight pennies they claimed were found in the well. The Old Dame sent them back immediately, saying she would not have Piskeys in her house for untold gold.

He also reports a local belief that if 'anyone should visit the well without leaving an offering, they would be followed home by a cloud of Piskeys in the guise of small night-flying moths, believed to embody spirits of the dead'. (Langstone, 2017, p.37)

Today the site remains one of the most special holy wells in all of Cornwall. The carved design on the basin is hidden by a luxurious cloak of liverwort. The bowl of water shines sparkling and clear. All around the basin are offerings, little statues of Fairies, Leprechauns and winged figurines, indicating the well is still lovingly tended to (2024).

Quiller-Couch records the following story, which bears great resemblance to a tale told of St Cuby's Well in Duloe.

An old farmer remembered that long-forgotten granite basin and had always liked the look of it. It was made beautifully, but he did not covet it for himself; he needed a trough for his pigsty and saw no problem using the holy font. It was made to hold water after all.

He took his oxen down the lane to the well and fixed chains around the granite basin. He tried to dislodge it by hand, but there was no chance of moving it. The thing even resisted the tugs from his oxen, but after pushing them harder and harder, finally, the granite bowl shifted out of its ancient home and they slowly pulled it up the hill to where the cart was waiting.

Just as they reached the cart, the basin broke free from the chains and rolled down the hill, making a sharp left, rolling back down the steps into its own old place, beneath the gentle drip of the spring water.

The old man couldn't believe what he had witnessed, but the old story of the well being haunted by a Piskey came back to him. He decided to leave it well alone, and retreated back to his oxen, but found them both dead. He told his story that night, but the next day he could no longer walk and was speechless for the rest of his days.

No one has ever tried to move the basin since.

THAT'S ENOUGH TO GO ON WITH

Somerset

Have you had enough?
Have you had too much?
Have you given thanks?

Once upon a time, there was a little boy and a little girl who had lost their mother and father, so they lived with their grannie. They never had enough to eat, but their grannie had taught them good manners and people liked them for it. Some would give them a cabbage leaf, others would give them some scrumpy, other neighbours would give them a turnip, or a pot of bones for soup or stale crust that the hens had left over … Whatever it was, they would always say, 'No more please. That's enough to go on with, thank you kindly.'

There was a fat, rich farmer who lived close by who had well-stocked orchards and corn ricks that were always full. His fields boasted the finest cows, and he knew about the poverty around him, but he never spared a single cabbage leaf nor a taste of meat for his neighbours (that would have cost him money.)

He grew richer and richer and fatter and fatter.

One day the little girl and the little boy took their little goat to grass. They had to go along a lane near the farmer's field and when they looked over into that field, the rich man's dog started barking. The old miser followed them, throwing stones at them until they rounded the corner. His aim hit their old grannie as she was picking up twigs on her own little plot. He called her a witch and accused the children of stealing his cow's milk, which was a terrible lie.

'We have our own goat for milk, thank you very much,' she said, rubbing the bruise forming on her neck.

After that, the old lady told the little boy and the little girl that perhaps they shouldn't go anywhere near the old man's fields.

For days and weeks and months, they took the goat the longest paths to find grass that wasn't near the farmer's land. One day the little goat broke free and ran into the enchanted wood, where the grass grew green and the Little Men lived.

No one ever went into that wood and they were frightened, but the little boy and the little girl knew they had to get the little goat out quick. They remembered their good manners and said, 'Please, forgive our hungry goat, may we come into your wood and catch her? Thank you kindly.'

In they went and followed her path through the grasses and plants, but she wasn't eating grass. She was eating strawberries. As quickly as she could. The wood was filled red with them.

The little boy and the little girl stopped and gave each other a hungry glance, and at the same time spoke aloud, to the trees, 'We are very hungry and so is our grannie at home … May we pick a handful?'

The mischievous Little Men called out, 'Pick all you want!' The children did not know these strawberries were enchanted. If you ate one, you could not stop … until you gave thanks.

But Grannie had taught them well and after they had picked a double handful to take home, they said, 'That's enough to go on with, thank you kindly.'

As soon as they had said it, the goat stopped eating and came up to them and they were all able to make their way out of the woods safely.

They went home and shared the strawberries with their grandmother and the goat, and all of them were delighted. They never went short of milk after that. And the curious thing was, from that day on, strawberries grew in their garden all year round, so they never went hungry again.

In the midst of winter, the farmer happened to walk past their little garden and saw the red strawberries growing against the white snow.

'You stole the strawberries from my wood!' he screamed.

'No,' said the children, 'Those strawberries came from the Little Men's wood.'

'That wood belongs to *me*!' he continued to scream. Which was really unwise because the Little Men were listening.

He leapt over the garden gate and ate every single strawberry 'til they were all gone. But he had started, and now he wanted more, so he went over the wall into the Little Men's wood and ate more and more. There were so many strawberries lying against the snow, he ate handful after handful. He found he couldn't stop, even though he wanted to.

He ate more and more, and he couldn't say 'please' and he didn't know how to say 'that's enough', so he had to keep on eating. Of course, if he had only known how to say 'thank you kindly' it would have been fine, but he didn't, so he ate and he ate … all day, all night, all week, until Sunday came, when he burst with a bang.

9

THE TIME HAS COME: PIXIE REPARATIONS

It is not children only that one feeds with fairy tales.

Gotthold Ephraim Lessing

What if we have *not* been good neighbours?

What if we have *not* acted with best respect?

What are the consequences of our actions?

Is it too late?

Can we find a way to make amends?

In this chapter, we will meet various people who have had especially unfortunate encounters with the Pixies. With cause comes effect.

As we grow we learn we are entangled in a world of mutual responsibility. We depend on each other to survive and thrive and grow. We forget at our peril that in a system of reciprocity our actions affect others.

Very simply, the Pixies will hold us accountable. But, maybe there is still a chance to make amends? The trickster that holds the mirror to our behaviour allows us to notice our patterns and change our story.

Can you distinguish between what is real and what you believe to be real?

Step closer to your fear and you might find a Spriggan has swollen to the size of a Giant. It is not always an easy path to be vulnerable and honest, but sometimes all it takes is the ability to ask, 'What can I do to make peace?'

Change one word in a story and you might break a spell.

There is still more to find in the fairy tale.

SPRIGGANS OF TRENCROM HILL

West Penwith, Cornwall

It has been a long time since the age of Giants in Cornwall. Some of their legends like 'Jack the Giant Killer' are thought to date back 5,000 years, which is pretty amazing, particularly as they are still told today. In the days when the Giants started to be slaughtered by the incoming conquerors, they hid their treasures of gold and jewels between the shadows of granite at Trencrom hill, or, as they knew it, Trecrobben. They secured their hoards with such potent spells they are kept safe to this day. The Spriggans guard the hill still, for they know the imaginations of men get greedy.

On Midsummer's Eve 2024 I walked up Trencrom Hill to watch the sun set. Farmers in neighbouring fields were busily bundling hay into round bales. I stood and watched the final golden light stretch across West Penwith, all the way to the hazy horizon hiding the Lizard. It felt to me that the treasures of Cornwall were on grand display.

Once upon a time, there was a man who had a dream that somewhere in Cornwall there was a hill filled with treasure. He travelled around the county and kept his ear out for any talk of hill-hidden gold. There was an old droll teller who lived on the cliff in Lelant. He knew old stories, they said.

He found the droll teller by the hearthside of an inn, telling traditions and stories to a captive audience. The man asked the droll teller if he knew any tales of hills with hidden treasure.

The old droll teller gave him a careful look. He told the tale of the treasure at Trencrom Hill. He finished it saying 'much of that treasure is said to still be there, safely held in that hill'. He looked back to the man who had asked for the story, and added, 'but a warning to all … the gold in that hill is fiercely guarded by the Small People.'

The next day, the man went to Trencrom Hill and he found it was exactly as he had dreamt.

He fetched a spade and returned to the hill under cover of darkness. As the night fell, the moon rose and he climbed the side of the enchanted hill with his spade and a big bag.

He scrambled across the rugged, rocky side of Trencrom Hill and became excited by the sense that the treasure was not far off. Perhaps the gold was whispering to him, yearning to be found. Were those diamonds calling to him, wishing to sparkle in the sun again?

As he climbed over the rocks of ancient cairns, the sky clouded over and held back the moonlight. He was left in unearthly darkness. In that moment, the wind rose and roared around him. He sheltered in the rocks, hoping the wind would blow over soon.

A huge crash of thunder announced an approaching storm. The land around him seemed to open and move, as if the gorse and fern and bracken were moving of their own accord.

Flashes of lightning followed in quick succession and in each flash the man perceived tiny Spriggans swarming from the rocks around him in swathes. Lightning flashed, flash after flash, and all the while more small folk came. They were terrible to look at, more like insects than anything else.

With each flash of lightning not only did their numbers increase but they grew in size, bigger and bigger until they towered over him in almost Giant form.

Grotesque faces stared him down with looks so terrible, so ferocious, that he was sure he was a goner.

He leapt into the darkness, away from their terrible grasping hands. How he escaped, he could never be sure. When he was discovered the next day he was so frightened, he did not come to his senses for a long while.

And so, the treasures of Trencrom Hill remain protected.

BARKER'S KNEE

West Penwith, Cornwall

Towednack, pronounced to-wed-nack, is a lovely spot, just outside St Ives. The church town of Towednack is at the base of super-steep Trendrine Hill and Rosewall Hill.

Both these hills have legends of Little People. The tale of Skillywidden (not included in this book) is from Trendrine and there are stories of Knockers working in Rosewall mines – perhaps they are the same spirits who appear in this story?

Once upon a time, in the Parish of Towednack, there was a man named Barker who was a pain in the bum. He didn't make many friends, which didn't bother him because he found he knew better than most people anyway. His neighbours were always talking about how hard the industrious Buccas worked, and it annoyed Barker, who was often quite idle himself.

One night they annoyed him more than ever. All the old boys were in the inn talking some nonsense about a sacred well where you could hear the Knockers.

'If you put your head to the ground, right by the water, the sounds of the spirits can be heard, hard at work. The knocking of their Fairy tools echo out through the water as they hit against rock again and again, day after day.

Another old boy chipped in, 'Well, not *every* day … Whether you know them as Buccas, or Knockers, or what, they stop their work to celebrate the Jewish Sabbath, Easter and Christmas celebrations.'

Barker told his neighbours they were stupid.

'Have you been to listen for yourself?' someone said.

'What a load of nonsense,' he replied. 'I *will* go, and I suspect I will hear nothing. And even if I do, I'll be able to find an explanation for it.

He visited the well, and much to his surprise, it *did* sound like there was a particular musical tinkering coming from the water.

He lay on the ground as close as he could get to the water, flanked by the fern that surrounded the well.

Amazed, he realised it *was* possible to make out voices. They were talking and laughing as they worked.

He started recognising their voices apart, and finally started catching their words.

The dappled shade grew warmer and warmer over the summer that year and the longer Barker spent at the well, the more he understood the pattern of their daily routine.

He knew exactly when they were going to start working. He could tell you when they would pause for lunch, and when they were going to stop after their eight-hour day. When they had finished, they would hide their tools in a new spot every day. They even chose to announce it, although he could not tell you who they were hiding them from.

'I'll leave my tools in the cleft in the rock,' said one voice that day. 'I'll leave mine under the fern,' said another, and a third said, 'I'll leave mine on Barker's Knee.'

He was surprised to hear his name, but at that very moment of recognition, an excessive pain exploded in his knee. It felt like a heavy weight had been dropped on him and remained within his knee cap.

'Take it away! Take it away!' he cried, in searing pain, with stars in his eyes.

His cries were answered by laughter rising from the spring.

From that day, to the day of his death, Barker had a stiff knee. He tried to hide the true cause from his neighbours, but they found out.

'Thats what happens when you don't respect the privacy of the Good Folk,' they said.

His story became so well known that 'as stiff as Barker's knee' became a proverb.

THE WOMAN WHO TURNED HER SHIFT

West Penwith, Cornwall

On Worvas Hill, overlooking Carbis Bay and St Ives, there stands a 50ft granite obelisk called Knill's Steeple or Knill's Monument. It was intended to be the mausoleum of John Knill, who was the mayor of St Ives from 1767 and was responsible for building the town's first pier during his time in office. The Cornishman *newspaper suspected him of privateering and claimed he was involved in the smuggling trade. He later made a fortune collecting taxes in Jamaica for King George III.*

It has become a prominent landmark used along the coast by vessels for navigation, and overlooks Penwith towards the Lady Downs and down to Penzance.

Before the hill was dominated by the obelisk, there was a tin miner's cottage where the monument now stands. The cottage stood alone among the tin country and was given the name Chy-an-wheal, which means 'House on the Mine'. There was talk that the Spriggans of Trencrom Hill favoured this place.

This is one of the tales where we see the Spriggans as loot-bearing plunderers. It was recorded by Hunt.

Back in those days, a widow of an old miner lived in the house called Chy-an-wheal. Her husband had died in a terrible accident in the open mine workings and she was left terribly poor. The people of St Ives saw her coming to market carrying on the best she could and were surprised when she bought little luxuries for herself as if she were some grand dame.

People talked, as they do. They said she was frivolous, they said she was making money in unknown ways, they said no good would come of it. There was definitely something suspicious about that woman.

They were quite right. She did have a secret.

Every night, when they thought she was sleeping, the Spriggans of Trencrom Hill crept into Chy-an-wheal and used it as their meeting place. They gathered together, opened their bags and shared their plunder. How the old lady had enticed them in or, if they had chosen the spot on their own accord, I cannot tell you, but as long as she was sleeping, it was clear that they felt brazen and brave in her house. As payment for her discretion, they left a coin from their treasure for her each night.

She lived very comfortably for one in her position. When she went into town she would buy a fancy bonnet or some sort of exotic fruit. She just loved glimpsing the shocked faces of those old gossips at market. She went home with a smile on her face, knowing they would be talking about her for days.

But she was unsatisfied with her fortune, or perhaps reckless, because she made plans to bide her time and become rich by these little spirits.

Lying in bed, she pretended to sleep and kept an eye on the Spriggans. She decided to wait for a night when they arrived with an unusually large amount of loot.

Soon enough, she watched beneath her sheets as piles of gold and jewellery glistened and gleamed on her kitchen table. It was the greatest haul she had ever seen.

With squeaking noises and guttural clicks, pointing and growling, the spirits began to quarrel over how they might split the bounty.

'Now is my time,' thought the woman under the covers. She was wearing her shift in bed, and knowing that an item of clothing turned inside out would command power over the spirits, very carefully, she took it off and turned the shift inside out and put it back on again.

She leapt from her bed and jumped into the centre of the room, stunning the spirits.

'None of you shall have a penny!' she roared, touching the treasure, which claimed it for the mortal realm. The Spriggans disappeared instantly. All except for one, who was the boldest of the lot. He looked at her and brushed his hand over the old woman's shift with a cruel smile before he vanished.

She was rich!

Oh, how those old gossips talked in the following days when that old poor widow bought one of the most fantastic houses in all of St Ives.

However rich she became, some strange affliction affected her terribly, for on random days and at random times, her body was tortured beyond endurance. She paid all sorts of money for doctors to come and see what the matter was, but although they used long and fancy words, none of the wisest minds in medicine had any idea why she was in such distress.

If only she had asked those old gossips on the market. They knew the work of the Spriggans when they saw it. If they had looked close enough at the shift she used to betray the Spriggans, they would have seen the curse embroidered into it, and known this was the root of her distress and undoing.

THE MAN WHO COINED HIS BLOOD TO GOLD

West Penwith, Cornwall

A lot of the stories of the Knockers have the cause and effect of reciprocity about them. In his chapter on Piskies and Knockers in Magical Folk *(Young & Houlbrook, 2023, p.155), Ronald M. James suggests that many of the Knocker stories date back to the days of the independent tribute miners, whose fortunes depended on the amount of tin they produced.*

The incentive behind tribute mining is clear: excite the miners (who were referred to as adventurers) to discover ore and raise it fast and cheaply. The disadvantage was that the tributes shared the risk of the activity and costs incurred, not to mention unknown hours of work. Mining trade unions generally opposed tribute mining.

During the rise of the British Empire, mining was a rich industry of innovation and national pride. Some did indeed make vast fortunes, but it was rarely the miners themselves.

The conditions in mines were appalling by modern-day standards, and profits were valued more than people. Death and injury were everyday occurrences.

The last working Cornish tin mine, South Crofty, closed in 1998, with a devastating effect on the local community, economy and landscape. Not long after it closed, the graffitied words of singer Roger Bryant appeared along the mine's outside wall: 'Cornish lads are fishermen and Cornish lads are miners too. But when the fish and tin are gone, what are the Cornish boys to do?'

The legacy and effects of mining are complicated, particularly for communities where they once thrived. Flooded mines contain high levels of metal-laden acidic water. Arsenic and other unwanted heavy metals were deposited in waste tips close to where they were extracted and continue to contaminate soils.

As this book goes to print, Cornish mining is facing a revival with a series of proposed lithium mines across the county. What lessons have we learned to protect people, community and land?

I found this story by chance in a second-hand bookshop in Truro. It speaks of the mining experience from a refreshing perspective. It is an authored tale, heavily inspired by mining folklore, published in Drolls from Shadowland *(1893) by Joseph Henry Pearce.*

This may be one you don't read to younger children before bed.

As he approached the entrance to the tunnel that would steal the daylight of yet another day, Joel made sure to swear into the grey skies for his cursed life. It was not wise for a miner to curse down there, in the subterranean underground. He feared the spirits that echoed their presence through the stone.

Poverty held him here. He thought it cruel of fate to show him so much of the riches underground and not allow him to keep much of it himself. The dreary darkness pressed down on his shoulder as he entered the tunnel. He brooded moodily as he hunched, stumbling down the dark passageways of the adit, down to the shafts that would take him deeper down.

Among the continually dripping wet walls, he could hear the muffled echo of exploding rock in different areas of the mine.

He began the back-breaking work, picking his way into the rock.

'I'm sick to death of this life,' he muttered bitterly, wishing there was a way that he could free himself from the endless torment.

At that moment his pick hit the stone and to his surprise the wall gave way, revealing a darkness that no human had ever looked into before.

Jagged fragments lay about his feet, but the impenetrable gloom transfixed him. It must be a trick of his imagination, but that darkness looked like it sparkled.

He drew his candle nearer, passing his head through the opening.

Dark sparkling crystals coated the crust of this little grotto. But his heart leapt as the shadows between the rock moved of their own accord. A blotch of shadow drew into the bent form that looked somewhere between a little man and a weasel. It stood on two legs and held its own little pick. It stepped up to the opening in the rock and regarded Joel.

'What can I do for ee friend?' the crooked creature asked with a voice so faint that it sounded like it was coming from a very far distance.

Joel's jaw dropped as he stared at this tiny little man.

'What can I do for ee?' repeated the crooked man.

Joel moistened his lips. 'Nothing, pray sir,' he stumbled.

'Nonsense my man,' said the little man cheerfully, rubbing long and bony hands together. Sparkling rings bejewelled his skinny fingers.

'I am your friend. If you will let me be …' A sparkle flashed in his deep dark eyes.

'Come! Don't be put off by my appearance. In what way can I oblige thee, friend? I can grant you any wish you like. Is it money you need? It is, isn't it?' The little man spoke as if this were a question, but smiled and said, 'I could hear your heart wishes before the stones fell, friend.

Change of scenery you want? Say the word and it will be done. Pile of coins could be useful eh … boy?'

'How do you come to know so much?' said Joel, anxious.

'I know more than that. I know you don't have much saved, I know you have dreams of getting out of this darkness. Better life for yourself? Just reach out and grab it! It's what I can give you.'

He began to chuckle to himself.

'Well, yes … I should like that.'

'Then give me your hand on it, comrade, and you shall have it all.'

'Here goes then,' gulped Joel, offering out his hand.

The crooked creature seized his hand and with its sharp grimy claws, dug them into Joel's wrist.

'Oh! Stop! Let go! Let go!'

'I won't be nasty to ee comrade! Every drop of blood you choose to shed for the purpose shall turn into a golden coin for ee!'

'Your nails … you're hurting me!'

The claws of the creature dug in deeper and harder. A drop of blood started pooling under the crooked man's nail.

'Try the charm, man. Wish. Hold your arm out and say – Wan.'

Joel broke free from the creature's grasp. He gasped in revulsion, holding out his arm as the blood oozed.

'Wan!' he said as the drop fell to the ground in that darkened cavern.

The moment the blood touched the ground a glimmer of gold glittered and the tinkle of metal echoed in the chamber. Joel picked up the coin and bit it.

'This is gold. Real gold.' He stashed it in his pocket for safe keeping.

'I told ee. Try again,' the smiling creature encouraged, 'Make up a pile.'

Joel put out his arm and watched the next drop of blood collect. 'Wan!'

As the blood touched the earth, another coin sounded at his feet.

'Try again,' said the little man.

'Wan!' he called, louder and more eager.

'Wan! Wan! Wan!'

The gold coins glittered on the ground and as Joel's eyes grew bigger, the crooked man sunk back into the shadows, watching intently.

Joel grew giddy with the excitement of all that gold shining at his feet.

'Wan! Wan! … Wan!'

Joel found himself leaning on the corner of the rock to support himself, light-headed. He repeated the words. He didn't know how much he would need, but he didn't want to stop yet.

'Wan … wan … uh … wan …'

Without realising, he slipped and fell, unconscious, on the pile of gold coins as the crooked man appeared out of the shadows once more, rubbing his hands.

'Not long now,' said the little man, waiting at Joel's mouth.

A little yellow flame danced out of Joel's throat and fluttered rather anxiously up to his lips. The flame seemed to have its own consciousness as it moved, searching for something. The gold coins glowed beneath the flame's light. It flickered in terror as those sharp claws closed around it.

'Not such a bad bargain after all,' chuckled the crooked man and all was cast into darkness once more.

OLD FARMER MOLE

Exmoor, Somerset

There are three things you can be certain that an Exmoor pony can do: climb up a steep cleeve, carry a drunkard and see a Pixy.

Old Farmer Mole was a beast of a man. He was a terror for staying at the pub 'til he had spent all the coins he had made at market. How his poor wife survived with those children nobody knew.

He would go home with empty pockets and a breath full of cider, so that his poor pony would have to manage its own way home, balancing its swerving, swearing, singing rider.

One night he fell off his poor pony and spent the night in the ditch. It deserved him right, of course. In the morning, he made his way home and beat his wife black and blue in front of the children, so they would learn, too. He scalded her for not staying up to ensure his safe return.

The Pixies knew something needed to be done. They thought to scare the pony, but Mole's pony was so sure-footed it was no use.

A mist rolled in just as Old Farmer Mole was leaving the pub, steaming with cider as usual. The pony knew what to do and started the journey home.

Old Farmer Mole looked out and saw a lantern held up into the air on the path in front.

'That wife of mine thinks she's going to escape a beating by bringing out a torch. I'll beat her for leaving the children!'

But the pony moved away from the light, finding its own path.

Farmer Mole tried to stop the pony and turn it towards his wife.

The pony refused its master. It could see the light was a Pixy, holding a lantern standing atop the blackest bog.

Farmer Mole took out his whip and made sure the pony knew to follow the light to his wife. The pony resisted, but Old Farmer Mole … was very convincing. The pony stepped into the bog up to its ankles, dug its feet in and refused to take a step further.

Old Farmer Mole slid off the pony and walked towards the light. Something cracked him on the head and he stumbled. He hadn't gone far when he toppled over and the bog swallowed him.

The old pony trotted home. When Farmer Mole's wife saw the empty saddle and the peat muck on the pony's ankles, she knew exactly what had happened. The first thing she did was to fetch a pail of fresh water and leave it out for the Pixies. Then she swept the hearth, and then she woke up the children and they danced.

The farm prospered from that day on.

10

WHEN PIXIES MEET: THE BALANCE OF ALL THINGS

We have had many encounters with the Pixies now. We have seen much mischief, we have peeped into other worlds, we have been lost, confused and beguiled. We have been led astray and we have stepped into Pixy-rings. Our neighbours have laughed with us and at us. It's not over yet …

As different as we are, we have also seen that humans and Pixies share some things in common. We both like to dance, and to laugh, to play games and pull pranks. We can both be capricious and cutting and fired by wrath. We are about to see in this last chapter that we both defend what we love.

Will anything make sense again?

Will we make it out alive?

What if we get stuck between both worlds?

'Between both' was a popular adage in Cornwall. The story behind it takes us to St Just.

Loafing around the public house on a payday, Bucca happened to pop his head into the room where Captain Chynolds and another gentleman were talking in a window seat. The captain looked up at the intruder and said, 'Which art thee, Bucca, a fool or a rogue?'

Before making any reply, Bucca placed himself between them and answered, 'I'm between both, I believe.'

KING OF PEW TOR

Dartmoor, Devon

This story appears in a couple of places, but the earliest I have found it is in Tales of the Tors *by A.G. Skinner, 1939. The book is a collection of folk tales retold, but this story feels more modern than ancient.*

Over the years I have worked with the story and made it my own in various ways, including the addition of the poem. Within the story we meet an ingenious Fairy called Gossamer, who uses her tears to spectacular effect. I have always enjoyed overemphasising the power of her Fairy tears (beyond the original source).

The first time I told this tale on location at Pew Tor, I was telling stories on a story walk organised by Emma Cunis, who runs Dartmoor walking company Dartmoor's Daughter.

Emma picked up on the Fairy tears and after the story, she took us all to a pool of water that stands permanently at the base of Pew Tor. Maybe these are the remnants of the Fairy tears? Emma then told us all of the work of Tom Greeves, who has a fascinating theory that some pools found on Dartmoor might have been designed in prehistoric times, whether for practical or religious functions, various pools align with cairns and stone rows. An excellent way to end the story.

I recommend visiting Pew Tor, it is a suitably grand residence for a Pixie King. Don't forget to leave an offering for the Pixies, but whatever you do don't leave litter.

For the Pixie King. May his tales continue to be told.

There was once a postwoman called Meg who spent her life carrying the post and newspapers to the houses and farms all around Moortown on the western side of Dartmoor. She spent her days walking miles and miles to deliver those letters.

Wherever she went, she was warmly welcomed and listened to whoever she met. She would pass on the scraps of gossip ('newsom' as it is known on Dartmoor) and in a way, she kept her community connected.

She walked a lot and visited the same places repeatedly, so she got to know those pathways very well. She felt into things, she was a good listener after all.

There were stones she walked past that had a special sort of presence, and bridges that felt like they bridged more than just the streams.

She left acorn cups and bits of biscuit at some of these places, just to mark them as special places.

But after a lifetime of walking, sciatica demanded that she give up her job and eventually she was bedridden. She became a lodger in the house just below Pew Tor with a kind family, who brought her food and tidied her room. She knitted to keep herself busy and started selling her creations to get by. 'There is always a way to get round a problem,' she would say to herself. Luckily the view out of her window looked out on to Pew Tor, and it continually reminded her how blessed she was.

There were stories that the King of the Pixies kept his residence at Pew Tor and she felt he must be the happiest Pixie in the world to live in such a beautiful spot.

However, at that very moment, the King of the Pixies was not happy. Not happy at all.

Within the depths of Pew Tor, the King had called all the Dartmoor Pixies into a high council to discuss a very serious problem.

Humans.

More and more, humans did not believe in magic, and yet they destroyed magic in their vast ignorance. The Pixies had never seen their King more furious.

'I've had enough. The most magical Pixie locations are being trampled upon, defiled and destroyed. The amount of rubbish being left in my palace at Pew Tor is offensive. *And,* in our most famous trysting place, a human tore off a flowering hawthorn branch and tried to burn it green. *Burn it! In bloom.*'

The King was blind with rage. 'The water, air and land are all being poisoned … Earth is suffering! We have to do something.'

With a wild look in his eyes, he declared war.

Unleash fury in your magic!
Weave it feral, make it tragic!
Pinch the children black and blue!
Try to drown the adults too!
Shine your lights into their eyes!
Don't stop 'til every human cries!
Pixy-lead them, into the mire!
Walk them backwards through the briar!
Steal their keys, their clothes, their hopes!
Time to teach these stupid dopes!
Create chaos never seen before!
Make this my magnificent Pixie War!

The Pixie King thought for a moment and smiled menacingly … 'Oh, and one more thing … I don't want any more chickens laying any more eggs. No more pancakes, no more omelettes … no more breakfasts. Nothing!

'Unleash your worst, Pixies.'

What fun they had! Mischief and mayhem played out on an unprecedented scale.

The Pixies played tricks on every single person across Dartmoor; visitors, residents, old, young, no one was safe. Cries and shouts, whimpering and wailing could be heard in every home, garden, hill and valley.

The Pixie that arrived at Meg's window lived in a special stone and knew her well. She had always left a biscuit when she had passed. The Pixie did not want to punish her too harshly. Instead it unravelled her balls of wool and tangled them over every fixture in her room.

When Meg woke up she saw the chaos. She heard the children crying and when she found that the adults were insensible or missing, she knew something was very wrong.

All across Dartmoor, no one was able to find their clothes, all the farmers found their milk was sour and no one had any eggs to sell.

But Meg was bed-bound, what could she do?

She held a tiny acorn cup in her hand and instinctively she made it into a ring. She held it to her mouth and spoke. 'Oh please, spirits of the land, we need your help.' She threw the cup out of the open window, and it was gone.

In Fairyland, Queen Mab was delivered the gift of wild hope wrapped up in an acorn cup.

'It's from Dartmoor, my Queen,' said a Fairy called Colin.

Mab sent her best emissary, Gossamer, to cross the border into Pixieland and investigate what was going down on Dartmoor.

The King of the Pixies was wild with glee. The war was going very well.

Those humans were finally feeling the wrath that they so very well deserved.

But, as Gossamer was sighted approaching Pew Tor, the King's good mood was dampened.

The tensions between the Pixies and the Fairies are very well known and a truce is held in a fine balance. The King called for the customary primrose tea and grasshopper ham to be served, and he greeted Gossamer with all formalities.

'Queen Mab is not best pleased with your dealings with the humans. She requests that you stop the war,' Gossamer said.

'I don't care what Queen Mab thinks. This is Pixieland! Besides, surely you agree the humans deserve it?'

'Queen Mab requests that you end the war,' said Gossamer calmly, ignoring the King's insult.

'I will not stop. If the humans can't see the magic that's in front of them, then maybe they shouldn't be able to see anything at all? They have brought about their own downfall,' he shouted.

'For the last time, Queen Mab asks you to stop the war,' said Gossamer calmly and firmly.

'This conversation is over. You can leave now, you stupid Fairy,' the Pixie King said furiously.

Gossamer stood up calmly, 'Queen Mab will be so very sad to hear your decision.'

The King turned away and Gossamer started to cry.

Fairy tears do not fall, they rise, and soon streams of tears floated in the throne room, heavy with threat.

'What are you doing?' said the Pixie King.

Gossamer looked at the King of the Pixies with a wry smile. 'Stop the war!' she demanded.

A single tear plummeted to the ground and unleashed an extraordinary amount of water across the floor.

'How dare you! You're making a mess. Stop it at once!'

'Stop the war,' pressed Gossamer as another tear shot to the ground, unleashing a wave the size of a swimming pool across the Pixie's palace.

'Stop this!' cried the King, standing on his table to get his feet out of the tears.

Another tear landed and another and another, until eventually the water rose up to the Pixie King's chin.

'Stop it you troublesome Fey!' he called as the water spilt into his mouth.

'Call back all your Pixies, tell them to undo this mayhem. Let your magic inspire insight and change, not harm and grief!' Gossamer spoke with grace and power and poise.

'Fine! Just put my palace back together.' The King grumbled his acceptance and the water poured out down the hill.

The Pixies were called back and undid their tricks. The children stopped crying and the adults found their way out of the ditches and mires and everything went back to how it should be.

Meg's wool was untangled and bundled up and a Pixie enchantment was woven into the threads, so that every jumper she knitted from that day forth kept out even the most biting Dartmoor wind. They became extraordinarily popular at Tavistock market.

All was put right, and the Pixies were ordered to leave treasures of wisdom, enchantment and knowledge upon the paths of the humans, and those who found them discovered the most incredible blessings. However, it did not stop the Pixies pulling tricks on anyone who ignored them.

Ever since that day, a pool of water has remained at the base of Pew Tor to remind the King of the Pixies of the promise he made.

A few days after everything had been put right, a farmer's wife noticed that the chickens had not laid an egg since all the strangeness had happened. A Pixie was sent to undo the charm on the chickens. As soon as it was done, the chickens all over Dartmoor started firing eggs out of their backside with a 'pew pew pew pew pew pew pew.'

GOBLIN COMBE

North Somerset

If you were looking for magic, you have come to the right place. This story reveals the keys into Fairyland … primroses.

But be warned. With the wrong amount of primroses, there's no way out. But the right amount? Party of your life and the greatest gifts to go home with.

Such is the power of the primrose.

I am a Goblin and primrose lover, so this is a firm favourite. This story is from a place of the same name, north of the Mendips, not far from Bristol Airport. This does mean it is outside the River Parrett Pixieland/Fairyland border, but remains in Somerset. It was introduced to me by Lisa Schneidau in her brilliant Botanical Folk Tales *(2018). I love her version, so have drawn from it. It was originally collected by Ruth Tongue.*

The children were told to stick together. The littlest was only 3 at the time, but you know children. Once they were in the wood, and picking the flowers for their Mammies, their attentions drifted.

The little one grabbed handfuls of primroses, more and more 'til her hands attracted bees. She followed the primrose path all the way down. How could she have known? She wandered straight down into Goblin Combe.

When it dawned on her that she was alone, the tears welled up in her eyes. She sat down on that big stone, the primroses plonked down next to her, and she cried and cried.

She wasn't aware of the sound the primroses made when they touched the granite stone, nor did she feel the stone shift open beneath her, nor did she notice the Little Folk who came out of the ground to inspect what all the hullaballoo was about.

The Fairies came to comfort her. They brought out a golden ball and they made a game of it. Her tears were still running down her face when she started laughing. The game went on and on and on, until her eyes couldn't stay open any longer and she sat back on that big stone and fell asleep.

She woke in her bed, surrounded by primroses and that golden ball in her hands. Her siblings had been scolded for abandoning her. Soon the extraordinary story and golden ball were all the family could speak about. Soon all the village knew.

A man listened to the story with keen ears. He was out the next day, picked a few primroses and had the most harrowing journey to find that big stone in Goblin Combe. Finding it at last, he sat down, wondering how much gold he would return home with.

But it was not the right day, and he hadn't picked the right amount of primroses, and he wasn't the right one, so they took him, and he was never seen again.

FAIRY FAIR

Blackdown Hills, Somerset

Tales of a Fairy fair witnessed in the Somerset hills date back to 1684 when Richard Bovet published the account of Mr Edmund Anstey in his work Pandaemonium, or the Devil's Cloister.

In the account, Anstey is returning home one dark night from Woodbury Hill. His horse is spooked and rushes violently, snorting and trembling along a bank.

Anstey heard 'the hedges crack with a dismal noise' and in front of him on the road appeared a 'circle of duskish light, the size of a very large wheel'.

In the centre of the circle was a terrifying bear with a pair of flaming eyes (Bovet, 1684).

There are later accounts in which people claimed to have seen the fair in 1856 and again in 1926, but both times the witnesses dared not approach.

Another story told to Ruth Tongue describes a man near Wellington seeing a 'Pixy Vair'. This time there were market stalls and the plucky man saw a golden cup among the revelling spirits. He rode his pony headlong into the gambolling spirits, grabbed the cup (and all the gold it contained.) and bolted home faster than he had ever ridden before.

Upon waking the next morning, the cup had turned into a 'gert toadstool.' When he checked his pony, he discovered she was lame, and she was until the end of her days.

The following story was compiled by Ruth Tongue from fragments heard from two sources in Bishop's Hull in 1905 and Milverton in 1910.

There was a farmer who once walked straight into a Fairy market and he even got home safe!

The last light of day spilled out around him as he walked through the fields home. Suddenly the Fairies' fair was around him, full of stalls filled with wonders beyond imagination.

On one stall the farmer saw a leather cider mug, and asked how much it was.

Getting out his money bag, he handed them a coin and the Fairies gave him a heap of dried leaves as change. He took the leaves quite seriously and wished them 'Good-night arl'.

When he and his wife went to bed they left the mug on the table, surrounded by the dead leaves. Of course, neither of them expected to see the treasures in the morning, but both of them went to sleep that night knowing the experience alone was worth its weight in gold.

You can imagine how surprised they were the next morning when they entered the kitchen to see the cider mug had been turned to solid silver and the leaves all around it into lumps of gold.

You can mark my words that every night afterwards, for the rest of his days, the farmer left a fresh pail of well water and some scalded cream out on his hearth in gratitude.

FAIRY FORT

Exmoor, Somerset

We have seen that the Fairies and the Pixies do not always get on. There are many personalities, opinions and troubles that brew between neighbours. Family is a strange magic. Relating can get sticky.

Sometimes, bigger problems arrive that, against all the odds, enable us to come together and weave a magic beyond our wildest dreams.

This story was recorded by Revd George Tugwell in 1863. He heard it from a moorland peat cutter who lived on Exmoor. I have retold it for our times.

The Dwarfish Earth spirits lived deep under the wild hills of Exmoor and its borders, for they did not like the light of the day, nor the stars of night. They were powerful and terrible, and it was better for all that they remained beneath the roots of the moors.

The Pixies and Fairies preferred to be around and near the surface, by day or night, so peace was normally held. But peace did not last.

One day, a very long time ago, the Dwarfish Earth spirits waged war with the Little Folk on the surface of Exmoor. Why it was so, we can only guess, but the Dwarfish Earth spirits made a ferocious attack. It seemed they wanted to control the surface. Some said they wanted to steal the stars.

The Fairies are a force to be reckoned with and the Pixies are formidable too, but the surprise attack of the Dwarfish Earth spirits forced all the powers of Faerie and Pixie to retreat. The huge power of the ill-tempered subterranean spirits overpowered the delicate ecosystems on the surface like bulldozers among bluebells. What were they to do? They fled and went into hiding to survive. The Dwarfish Earth spirits took the surface, they stole the stars.

After a while hidden away, the Faerie Queen decided she'd had enough. Was she not endlessly resourceful? Was she not daring, bold and brilliant? They might be small, but was that not a particularly potent part of their power? Was she not a woman? She knew her power and knew she had to fight.

The Faerie Queen considered the most powerful tools of the Little Folk: they had Three, Seven, Running Water and the ever-powerful Circle.

She called to her Fairies, 'I have a plan, but it will need everyone's help. Find the Pixies!'

The Pixies and the Faeries gathered together. There was curiosity between both parties. What was the Faerie Queen up to?

'Together! We must weave our magic together. Remind the earth why we have the right to be here!' She held aloft a circle in the air above her to make her point. She cried out to all the star worshippers, 'We must build a great circle on top of the highest hill.'

The site was an extremely strong position, carefully chosen by the Faerie Queen. It overlooked the valleys of three rapidly moving streams and commanded views in seven different directions.

The Pixies could see the genius of her idea, so got to work. Together with the Fairies, they built a magical, giant, circular fort. As you might expect, it was no ordinary structure. They sang a song into a circle that raised the stone and the turf around them into a protective ring. Into this spell each magical being wove their own experience of love for the earth.

A circular song of living memory, of loving relating was planted into the ground. Words of magic, for place and plant, stone and star, cloud and river and storm. Favourite things of the Fairies and the Pixies were enchanted into the spell again and again.

They called forth their favourite songs and stories, memories and best spells, powerful words, kindest deeds, strongest relations. All were woven into the ground and enchanted the structure. There were so many of them lending their help to this task that the giant fort was finished before the sun set. The fort completed, the magic began to flow infinitely within the circle. The power emanated out in the seven directions, through the three valleys, and was lifted by the running water. Charged magic was carried across the land. The whole of Exmoor became a stronghold of magical intent.

As the night fell, the Dwarfish Earth spirits drew toward the new power. But they could not penetrate the walls of the fort. They were baffled by the woven spells. They roared with fury and frustration, they trampled and trod and raved with rage, attempting to undo the spells.

They could not break it. The fury they felt dampened as they danced, and as dawn rose across the wide expanse of Exmoor, the swirling mists parted to reveal the wild solitude of the highest places. Exhausted, the Dwarfish Earth spirits turned and receded back down into the darkness that they knew.

The Little Folk cheered and made great celebration, but the wisest wondered, how long would it last? The dark forces were bound to return again. Would they ever be safe?

The Little Folk watched as ring after ring of the faintest vapour lifted up from the protection of the fort and floated into the brightening sky. As the sun rose, light, safety and peace were woven into each enchanted ring.

The Little Folk watched the vapour rings continue to issue forth from the fort, blowing across the skies from Exmoor, to every place where magic lived.

Each spell of memory, story and song travelled on the wind hither and thither and landed wherever the grass grew greenest, wherever the streams ran merrily, wherever the sunlight fell brightest and the moonbeams boldest.

The mist circles vanished quickly, but wherever they landed a green ring of verdant grass grew. They flourished and grew year on year, and within each circle the Pixies and Fairies knew they were as safe there as they had been in that wonderful fort.

The Dwarfish Earth spirits have not yet returned to Exmoor.

Pixies leapt for joy, 'Take that suckers.'

Fairies cheered, saying, 'The stars are for everyone.'

A puckish little spirit said, 'Even the biggest problems can be solved by a little dance.'

BIBLIOGRAPHY AND FURTHER READING

There are many Pixies I have not had space to include among these pages, many of these tales are worth finding! For more insights and traditions of the Pixies and the wider Fae family, these sources have been endlessly helpful to me.

Baring-Gould, Sabine, *A Book of Dartmoor*, 1900

Baring-Gould, Sabine, *The Vicar of Morwenstow, a life of Robert Stephen Hawker*, 1876

Bray, Anna, *A Peep at the Pixies; or, Legends of the West*, 1854

Bray, Anna, *A Description of the part of Devonshire Bordering on the Tamar and the Tavy; its natural history, manners, customs, superstitions, scenery, antiquities, biography of eminent persons, etc. in a series of letters to Robert Southey*, 1836 (three volumes)

Bottrell, William, *Traditions and Hearthside Stories of West Cornwall* (three volumes), 1870

Bottrell, William, *Stories and Folklore of West Cornwall*, 1997

Bovet, Richard, *Pandaemonium, or the Devil's Cloister*, 1684

Bramshaw, Vikki, *New Forest Folklore, Traditions and Charms*, 2022

Briggs, Katharine M., *A Dictionary of Fairies*, 1976

Briggs, Katharine M., *The Anatomy of Puck*, 1959

Briggs, Katharine M., *Folk Tales of Britain, Narratives, Book 2*, 1970

Briggs and Tongue, *Folktales of England*, 1965

Brown, Theo and Dewar, Stephen, *Ghostly Gold and Goblin Tunes*, 1968

Brown, Theo, *The Fate of the Dead*, 1979

Cheung, Theresa, *The Element Encyclopaedia of the Psychic World*, 2005
Causley, Charles, *The Puffin Book of Magic Verse*, 1974
Cockerton, Francis, *The Pixy Book*, 1996
Colling, Maria M, *Fables and Other Pieces in Verse*, 1831
Couch, Jonathan, *A History of Polperro*, 1871
Courtney, Margaret Ann, *Cornish Feasts and Folklore*, 1890
Coxhead, J.R.W., *Devon Traditions and Fairytales*, 1959
Crossing, William, *Folk Rhymes of Devon*, 1911, p.47
Crossing, William, *Gems in a Granite Setting*, 1905
Crossing, William, *Tales of the Dartmoor Pixies*, 1890
Dacre, Michael, *Devonshire Folk Tales*, 2010
Davies, Gilbert, *The Parochial History of Cornwall, Founded on the Manuscript Histories of Mr. Hals and Mr. Tonkin*, 1838
Dean and Shaw, *The Folklore of Cornwall*, 1975
Elworthy, Frederick Thomas, *The West Somerset Word Book*, 1886
Edwards, Gillian, *Hobgoblin and Sweet Puck, Fairy Names and Natures*, 1974
English Forests and Forest Trees, Historical, Legendary and Descriptive, 1853
Evanz Wentz, W. Y., *The Fairy Faith in Celtic Countries: The Classic Study of Leprechauns, Pixies, and other Fairy Spirits*, 1910
Friend, Hilderic, *Flowers and Flower Lore*, 1884
Froud, Brian and Lee, Alan, *Faeries*, 1995
Gray, Harold St George, *Report on the Wick Barrow Excavations, Part II*, Volume 54, 1908
Guardian, Wind in the Willows, www.theguardian.com/books/2010/mar/24/wind-in-the-willows-bonhams, accessed January 2025
Halliwell, James Orchard, Dictionary of Provincial and Archaic Words, 1846
Harrington, Christina Oakley, *The Treadwell's Book of Plant Magic*, 2020
Harte, Jeremy, *Explore Fairy Traditions*, 2004
Hawker, R.S., *Footprint of Former Men in Far Cornwall*, 1870
Hunt, Robert, *Popular Romances of the West of England*, 1865 (Two editions)

Hurley, Jack, *Legends of Exmoor*, 1973
Jacksties, Sharon, *Somerset Folk Tales*, 2012
King, R.J., *The Forest of Dartmoor and its Borders*, 1856, p.75
Kruse, John, *British Pixies*, 2021, p.16
Kruse, John, *The Derrick*, 2017
Langstone, Alex, *From Granite to Sea*, 2017, p.119
Lenihan, Eddie, *Meeting the Other Crowd*, 2003
Manning, Paul, 'Pixies' Progress: How the Pixie Became Part of the Nineteenth-Century Fairy Mythology', p.81 in Tolbert, Jeffrey, & Foster, Michael, *The Folkloresque: Reframing Folklore in a Popular Culture World*, 2016
Norman, Mark, *The Folklore of Devon*, 2023
Northcote, Rosalind, *Folklore Magazine*, Vol. 11, No. 2 (Jun., 1900), pp.212–17
O'Connor, Mike, *Cornish Folk Tales*, 2010
Palmer, Kingsley, *The Folklore of Somerset*, 1976
Pearce, Joseph Henry, *Drolls from Shadowland/Cornish Drolls*, 1893
Poole, Charles Henry, *The customs, superstitions, and legends of the county of Somerset*, 1877
Quiller-Couch, M., *Ancient and Holy Wells of Cornwall*, 1894
Rutley, Cecily, M., *Legends and Folk Lore of Devonshire*, 1932
Schneidau, Lisa, *Botanical Folk Tales of Britain and Ireland*, 2018
Sharman, V. Day, *Folk Tales of Devon*, 1952
Snell, Frederick John, *A Book of Exmoor*, 1903
Skinner, A.G., *Tales of the Tors*, 1939
Tongue, R.L, *Somerset Folklore*, 1965
Tregarthen, Enys, *Pixie Folklore and Legends*, 1968
Tregarthen, Enys, *North Cornwall, Fairies and Legends*, 1906
Tregarthen, Enys, *The Piskey-Purse*, 1905
Tugwell, George, *The North Devon Hand-book: Being a Guide to the Topography and Archaeology*, 1863
White, Rupert, *Fern Seed and Fairy Rings*, 2022
White, Rupert, 'This Charming Man: FT Nettleinghame and his Piskey-Empire', www.artcornwall.org/features/Rupert_White/Piskey-Empire.htm, accessed December 2024

Wise, John Richard D. Capel, *The New Forest its History and its Scenery*, 1863
Wright, Elizabeth Mary, *Rustic Speech and Folklore*, 1914
Young, Simon, *Ann Jefferies and the Fairies*, 2023
Young, Simon, *Enys Tregarthen of Padstow: A Neglected Cornish Folklorist and Fairyist*, 2023
Young, Simon and Houlbrook, Ceri, *Magical Folk, The History of Fairies*, 2023

RECOMMENDED PODCASTS

Boggart and Banshee: A Supernatural Podcast
Celtic Myths and Legends
Fabulous Folklore with Icy
Fairy Whispering
The Modern Fairy Sightings Podcast
The Piskie Trap

Since 1993, The Society for Storytelling has championed the ancient art of oral storytelling and its long and honourable history – not just as entertainment, but also in education, health, and inspiring and changing lives. Storytellers, enthusiasts and academics support and are supported by this registered charity to ensure the art is nurtured and developed throughout the UK.

Many activities of the Society are available to all, such as locating storytellers on the Society website, taking part in our annual National Storytelling Week at the start of every February, purchasing our quarterly magazine Storylines, or attending our Annual Gathering – a chance to revel in engaging performances, inspiring workshops, and the company of like-minded people.

You can also become a member of the Society to support the work we do. In return, you receive free access to Storylines, discounted tickets to the Annual Gathering and other storytelling events, the opportunity to join our mentorship scheme for new storytellers, and more. Among our great deals for members is a 30% discount off titles from The History Press.

For more information, including how to join, please visit

www.sfs.org.uk